For the longest time they sat there, looking at each other...

Then slowly he lowered his mouth to hers and kissed her once more, putting his arms around her. This time it was different. It was a deliberately sensual kiss that left nothing to the imagination. It overwhelmed Katrina completely. Max released her abruptly. Stunned, she watched him go, then anger rushed in. What the hell did he think he was doing? Did he think he could barge into her house, demand information, kiss her senseless, just like that? She took a deep breath. She was shaking all over. Apparently he did....

Ever since **KAREN VAN DER ZEE** was a child growing up in Holland she wanted to do two things: write books and travel. She's been lucky. Her American husband's work as a development economist has taken them to many exotic locations. They were married in Kenya, had their first daughter in Ghana and their second in the United States. They spent two fascinating years in Indonesia. Since then they've added a son to the family as well. They now live in Virginia, but not permanently!

KAREN VAN DER ZEE

Making Magic

Harlequin Books

TORONTO • NEW YORK • LONDON
AMSTERDAM • PARIS • SYDNEY • HAMBURG
STOCKHOLM • ATHENS • TOKYO • MILAN
MADRID • WARSAW • BUDAPEST • AUCKLAND

ISBN 0-373-11729-9

MAKING MAGIC

Copyright © 1993 by Karen van der Zee.

First North American Publication 1995.

CHAPTER ONE

KATRINA was spying. The man on the beach below sat in the powdery sand in the shade of a coconut palm. He had a sheaf of paper in his hands and a box with more papers next to him. He was reading very intently, scribbling on the paper now and then. Katrina wondered what he was doing.

He had thick, curly brown hair above an angular face with a prominent nose and a solid square jaw. Not a handsome face, but an eminently masculine one, a face to be reckoned with. Having shared the beach with him on occasion, she was familiar with his physical appearance, if not with any other aspects of his being. He had a tall, athletic body with wide shoulders, a broad chest covered with a light mat of hair, and strong, muscular legs. He was tanned all over and he moved like a man comfortable with himself. His most striking feature, however, was his eyes, which were an intense, cobalt-blue. He was, in short, a good-looking man. No, he was a gorgeous man. Not that she was interested. She'd had enough of gorgeous men. She'd been married to one.

Actually, Katrina was not spying. She was simply standing at her own window in her own villa, savouring a luscious Belgian chocolate while enjoying the view of the turquoise waters of the Caribbean, the palm-shaded beach, the azure sky. She had every right to be standing there enjoying the scenery. The man just happened to be part of the scenery. She couldn't help it, could she?

He was wearing nothing but a pair of short black swimming-trunks and he'd been sitting under the coconut palm for hours, which annoyed her. She wanted to go to the beach herself and sit and read, but she didn't want him there. She didn't want those piercing blue eyes dissecting her. Whenever he appeared on the beach when she was there, she'd leave. He made her uncomfortable and she wasn't sure why. Unfortunately, the small cove was not private property, so there wasn't anything she could do about his being there. She sighed and popped another chocolate into her mouth. It had a creamy hazelnut filling, one of her favourites. The box was almost empty. She'd have to ask somebody to bring her some more from Barbados or make a trip there herself.

The phone rang and she turned away from the enticing scenery with the man in it. Her brother's voice boomed over the line, clear as if he were next door rather than halfway across the world. London, or Paris, wherever he was these days, trying to rescue the family business.

Her brother was her only living relative, except for a distant cousin who had relocated to Brazil when the FBI expressed an interest in his business dealings.

'You're still there?' Tyler asked. A rhetorical question, obviously, since she was answering the phone. 'When are you coming out of hiding?' Not a rhetorical question.

'I'm not in hiding, Tyler.'

'You've been on that God-forsaken island for months! What else would you call it?'

'This is not a God-forsaken island,' she said, putting a good dose of indignation in her voice. 'This is paradise. It's very peaceful, very restorative.' And the living is cheap, she added silently.

Tyler snorted. 'Listen, I thought you'd be *celebrating*, for God's sake!'

'Don't be crude, Tyler. Bastian was my husband.'

'Do me a favour and don't give me the grieving-widow routine, sweetheart.' He sounded impatient.

Katrina's hands clenched around the receiver as guilt gripped her. She was a widow and she wasn't grieving. It sounded cold and unfeeling. She didn't want to be cold and unfeeling.

'Good God, Katrina! He wasn't worth it! Come back to New York and get on with your life. You're free. Finally.'

This was true. Free, and broke. Bastian had left her a cold heart, a lovely villa and a mere fragment of his once considerable wealth, but Tyler didn't know that and for the moment she had no intention of telling him. He had financial problems of his own. Their father had died of a heart attack six months ago, leaving the business on the brink of bankruptcy. Her financial future did not look good. Eventually she might even have to find a job. The problem was, what kind of job? She'd never worked in her life. Growing up rich and spoilt did not necessarily prepare you for life in the normal working world. However, it was an idea whose time had come, terrifying though it might be.

She'd come to St Barlow to regroup, to have some peace and quiet, to decide what course of action to take about her future. She liked the island. She liked the house—five bedrooms and baths; spacious, airy, living-room; large veranda banked by moorish arches; glorious views from all windows; a state-of-the-art kitchen; access to the beach in the tiny cove below, shaded by palms—in short, a fantasy house on a fantasy island. Fantasy, of course, depended on your perspective. There were no casinos, no nightclubs, no luxury hotels apart from the Plantation, which was a supremely expensive, supremely exclusive luxury resort for the supremely wealthy. Royalty and stars came to the Plantation to escape the rigours of celebrity—the paparazzi, the fans, the reporters, the autograph hunters.

Katrina liked the quiet life here well enough, but her brother would not understand. He was a man who needed the energy of big cities—the people, the traffic jams, the stockmarket. He thrived on coffee, doughnuts, martinis and smog.

'Where are you calling from?' she asked.

'London. I'm selling the house. I thought I'd let you know, just in case you decided to come and stay.'

'I wasn't planning to.' London in January? He had to be kidding.

'I also want to sell the house in New York. We can't afford to keep it. Do you mind?'

Did she mind? She felt her throat close. The New York house was her home, the place where she'd grown up, a huge, two-hundred-year-old mansion full of precious antiques and loving memories. It was empty of people now, the furniture shrouded in white, the servants gone. She swallowed at the constriction in her throat.

'Do we have to?'

'I don't see another way out.' His voice had softened. 'Unless...'

'Unless what?'

'Unless somehow you'd be able to bail us out.'

'I don't imagine you're talking about a couple of thousand, are you?' she asked, knowing the answer.

'More like a significant number of millions.'

She sighed heavily. 'I don't have it.'

'I was afraid of that.' He sounded resigned. 'I've heard the stories. That good-for-nothing husband of yours...'

'Stop it, Tyler.'

'How bad is it?' he asked.

'Oh, I'll manage,' she said bravely. She would have to, wouldn't she? She tore at her hair, which wasn't very satisfactory since not a single hair on her head was longer than an inch and a half and she couldn't get a good grasp.

'We're going to have to figure out what to do with the furniture and the artwork,' Tyler said. 'Unless you want me to get an auctioneer——'

'Tyler! You can't do that!' It sounded so undignified, so...*desperate*. But then, these were desperate times, she had to admit.

'Then you'll have to go to New York and handle it. Take what you want and dispose of the rest.'

It was not a joyful conversation, and when it was over she went back to the window and looked gloomily out over the small cove below. The man was still there, even though the sun had disappeared behind a dark bank of clouds. An afternoon rainstorm was brewing. She could see the palm trees swaying in the wind, but the man seemed oblivious until a sudden gust of wind attacked the pile of papers and blew them into the sand and bushes growing against the rocks.

He leaped to his feet to rescue them and Katrina laughed. She couldn't help it. She watched him as he retrieved the papers, his tall, muscular body moving smoothly. He was a great specimen of the male of the species, that was obvious. She already knew he was a strong swimmer; she'd seen him a number of times in the last couple of months. Perhaps he worked out as well, played tennis at the Plantation courts, did sit-ups at home. She visualised him doing sit-ups, bare-chested, stomach muscles flexing. No, this was not a constructive train of thought.

His villa was close by, just above hers perched on the cliffs, but they'd never actually spoken. When they accidentally met in passing, they exchanged nothing more than a polite greeting, and that was it. Not too friendly, she'd concluded, which was fine by her. He obviously wanted to be left alone. Good. So did she.

But he did have great eyes, so blue, so... hypnotising, and his thick brown hair sparked with dangerous glints of red in the sun. No doubt he had a volatile temperament. She could not help feeling a stirring of interest.

She watched him gathering up the sheets of paper. Then he straightened, throwing one more careful glance around the beach to make sure he hadn't missed a paper. His back was towards her, until suddenly he turned around and glanced up at her window, looking, it seemed, straight into her eyes. Her heart lurched in her chest. Had he sensed she'd been watching him?

She stood transfixed, looking back into his eyes for what seemed an endless, timeless moment. Finally she tore herself away from the window and went into the kitchen and made a cup of coffee. Her hands trembled as she scooped beans into the grinder, spilling some on to the counter-top. This was ridiculous! She'd come here to get away from men—lawyers, bankers, reporters, well-meaning friends and various meddlers involved in the nightmare of a few months ago. She wanted to be alone. She didn't want any man disturbing her heartbeat, her nerves, her peace.

A coconut rum cake with a creamy rum frosting sat on the counter and she cut off a generous piece and put it on a plate. Mrs Blackett loved baking, especially cakes and pies. She was good, but not as good as Katrina herself, who had several fancy cooking classes in France and New York under her belt. But Mrs Blackett didn't know that, and Katrina wasn't about to tell her. Why intimidate her, or hurt her feelings?

Mrs Blackett was an attractive island woman whose ancestral genes were a pot-pourri of African, Indian and Dutch. She wore neatly belted dresses, had a cheerful manner and loved singing hymns while going about her duties. She worked mornings only, fixing breakfast, doing the housework and the laundry, and making lunch if Katrina so desired. Katrina, who loved cooking, prepared her own dinner.

It grew ominously dark and a moment later the rain came pelting down, a copious, tropical downpour that drenched everything for a short time, then stopped as suddenly as it had started.

Coffee and cake close at hand, Katrina sat on the rattan sofa and opened her book. Ten minutes later she was still staring at the same page. All she could see in her mind's eye was the intense blue gaze of the man on the beach.

The next morning Katrina stood naked on the bathroom scales and stared glumly at the trembling needle. Not a pound. Not a single lousy pound. It wasn't fair! She got off the scales and stared at herself in the mirror and sighed heavily. Not a pretty sight, was it? It was downright frightening. Dr Whepple would not be happy if he could see her now, but she was trying her very best to follow his instructions.

'It's all your fault, Bastian,' she muttered. 'You've made a wreck out of me.' But Bastian was not there to hear and it wouldn't have mattered if he had. He would only have laughed cheerfully and cracked a joke. Bastian hadn't believed in having problems. He'd believed in having fun. Bastian MacKenzie, hedonist extraordinaire. In the end he'd had all the fun and she was left with all the problems.

Well, it would do no good to blame him. She was responsible for her own happiness. At least that was what the self-help pop-psychology books said. Take charge of your own life. Don't be a victim.

So, all right, she was trying to do that. Only taking charge of your life was a whole lot easier if you weren't emotionally and financially broke. Well, she did have some money in the bank and she wasn't exactly destitute. Poverty, after all, was a relative term. However, she could not indefinitely live off her present bank balance and she would eventually have to do something creative and productive to start supporting herself. With the family business in dire straits, there was nowhere to turn.

As far as her emotions were concerned, she'd have to nurse them back to health, find something to fill up her heart and her life.

'You're on your own, kiddo,' she said out loud at her reflection. The words had a dire sound to them.

What she needed was a little magic. Or a small light in the dark to point the way. Or a big, warm hug and a loving word. She sighed again. Oh, a fortune for a hug! She'd been widowed for only a few short months, but she'd been hugless and lonely for many long years.

Katrina pulled on a pair of baggy shorts and a loose T-shirt, grimacing at herself in the mirror. Go ahead, feel sorry for yourself, her inner self jeered. See how far that gets you. Nowhere.

After a leisurely breakfast she spent an hour in the garden, weeding and watering her herb seedlings. It was probably nuts to try to grow herbs here, but it didn't hurt anything, and it was certainly a restful occupation, very restorative for ravaged souls. It was encouraging to see the tiny, fragile plants reach so bravely up to the sun. Like me, she thought wryly, reaching for the sun.

Her grandmother's country cottage in upstate New York had had a large herb garden and she remembered the lovely scents, the butterflies, the wonderful, fragrant food laced with familiar and unfamiliar herbs. Her own mother, too, had grown many herbs in the mansion gardens, much to the chagrin of the gardeners, whose formal landscaping designs had not included the use of humble herbs spilling recklessly across neatly manicured paths and flowerbeds.

Katrina stared at the small basil plants and the greenery blurred before her eyes. 'Oh, Mom,' she whispered. 'I wish you were here. I feel so lonely. What am I going to do?'

She got up and wiped a muddy hand impatiently across her eyes, irritated with her own weakness. It was better to face life with laughter than tears. She put the water hose away and went back into the house.

She took a book, a cold drink and the rest of the chocolates to the beach and settled herself on a towel. Two hours later the book was finished, her cold drink was finished and the chocolates were finished. She had a quick swim, gathered up her things and headed to the path leading to the villa.

Something white caught her eyes. Something white in the bushes by the rocks. She peered into the greenery, bending over to retrieve a couple of sheets of paper. It looked as if they'd been wet and had dried again, and immediately she thought of the man chasing his papers yesterday afternoon. She perused the papers, the type that came rolling out of computer printers. The sheets were covered with double-spaced text and her gaze flew over the lines.

The man made my skin crawl. 'So what's your plan?'

He shrugged. 'Catch a plane for Caracas. Find out about Joe.' An evil smirk contorted his face. 'Do my duty.'

That was a laugh. I looked at his ugly face and said nothing. He looked uneasy. He knew I had power, but he was not sure if I intended to use it. Good. Let him sweat for a while. He tossed back the last of his whiskey and finally left, dragging his left leg. He hadn't told me what had happened, who had shot him, and where the money had come from. I didn't want to know. I didn't give a damn.

I stood in front of the window and finished my whiskey. She was there again on the beach.

I'd watched her now for a number of weeks and I had no clue as to who she was and what she was doing alone on the island. There was no one else with her. Sometimes she would leave for a few hours, but most of the time all she did was laze around on the beach, eat boxes of Belgian chocolates and read trashy novels. She had very short, very dark hair, and very large, very dark eyes. She was strange, elusive, silent, and as skinny as an alley cat.

Her heart hammered wildly. Her hand shook. Fury rushed hot through her blood.

'Skinny as an alley cat'.

She stared at the typed copy in her hand. It was like something out of a journal, or a novel. But what she had in her fingers was not a piece of fiction, was it? There was no doubt, no doubt at all who the skinny alley cat was. It was yours truly, Katrina MacKenzie, newly widowed, stressed-out and penniless.

He was writing about her. He'd been watching her and he was writing about her. Oh, God. She closed her eyes, fighting fury and panic.

She looked at the second page, her gaze racing over the lines, meaningless at first, then . . .

She was standing naked by the water's edge, a lovely vision in the silver moonlight. Quietly I moved through the sand towards her. She turned as if she sensed my approach and smiled that tantalising, mysterious smile that made my blood run wild.

Under my hands her skin was smooth as silk. Her breasts were full and firm, and she sucked in her breath when I cupped their warm weight in my hands. Her large eyes were pools of dark water, hiding secrets in their depths. I bent my mouth to hers, felt the hunger rise in me, the need to know her, to conquer the secrets of her being, to make her

Here the page ended. Her cheeks were hot with embarrassment. The need to make her what? She was trembling all over. Was this her too? The woman he was seducing? There was no way to know since the pages were not consecutive. Twenty-three pages of unknown content lay between the two she had in her hand.

Damn him! Who did he think he was?

Gathering up her things once more, she rushed up the path and into the house, pulled on a long crimson shirt over her bikini and raced back out of the house, clutching the two crumpled papers against her chest. His villa, partially obscured by a large almond tree and amethyst bougainvillaea, was further up the rocky path, and by the time she reached it she was out of breath and full of rage.

The door stood half-open and she knocked on it loudly, hearing unfamiliar music spill out of the interior, exotic, hypnotic. Not your basic Mozart or Beethoven, not your modern-day rock or pop. She stood for a moment, quite captivated by the sounds, then knocked on the door.

She tried to catch her breath as she waited, listening to the music as it rollicked seductively through the air. A violin, doing playful, sensuous things, backed up by a jazz band. She felt a little dizzy and she closed her eyes, taking in a deep, calming breath.

No one came to the door. She knocked again. The music was covering up her knocking. Opening the door further, she moved inside. To hell with him. She wasn't going back down the path now that she'd worked up this wonderful rage. It needed venting and he was going to get a full dose of it.

She noticed him almost as soon as she entered the house, in a room off to the right. The door was open and she saw him sitting at a computer desk strewn with paper. The room looked as if a tornado had hit it. There were papers and books everywhere, and photographs. Photographs tacked on large cork boards and spread out on another desk.

He didn't notice her. He was typing rapidly, his fingers flying across the keyboard with great expertise, his whole body showing total absorption.

Suddenly his hands stopped moving. His head jerked up and he turned sharply. 'What the hell——?'

'Excuse me for barging in but I knocked and no one came to the door.' Always the polite one, she was. So well-brought-up. So well-mannered. She'd come to rave and rant at him and instead she was apologising. The music wafted around her, stroking her senses, doing crazy things to her system, overwhelming her anger.

The man scraped his chair back and leaped to his feet like a tiger ready to spring. 'You have no damned business coming in here like this! Don't you see I'm working?'

'Sorry to disturb you,' she said nicely, meaning not a word of it.

He raked both hands through his hair and his bright blue eyes shot fire. 'You didn't *disturb* me, lady, you wrecked my god-damned concentration!'

That did it. He was mad at her, was he? Good!

'Too bad,' she said coldly.

He pointed at the door. 'Out, now.'

She glared at him and anchored her feet to the floor. 'I'm not leaving until I'm finished.' So brave, so stupid. The man was twice her size, he was furious, and she was antagonising him.

One dark brow shot up and his mouth quirked. He crossed his arms. 'You have two minutes.'

She held out the two pages. 'I found these in the bushes by the beach,' she said coldly. 'I believe they're yours.'

He took them from her and glanced at them. 'So they are,' he acknowledged. 'Is that why you had to come up here and drag me away from my work? For a couple of sheets of paper I can print out again if I need them? For God's sake, woman, haven't you got anything better to do? Well, no, I suppose not,' he answered himself.

Anger swelled in her with renewed force. 'Perhaps you ought to ask yourself if *you* don't have anything better to do!'

'And what is that supposed to mean?'

'What the hell do you think you're doing writing about me?' Her voice shook with righteous indignation. 'How dare you write about me?'

His thick brows lifted fractionally. 'Write about you?'

'I can read! And I can add one and one together!'

He glanced down again. 'Oh, I see.' His mouth curved. 'This is not about you. It's purely fiction.'

'Sure it is! "She had very short, very dark hair",' she quoted. ' "She was skinny as an alley cat". Do you think I'm stupid?'

'I don't have an opinion one way or the other about your intellectual prowess, not knowing who you are.'

He didn't know who she was, he said. It was possible. Lots of people in the world didn't know who she was.

On the other hand, lots of people did know. Bastian had been much in the public eye, mostly in the tabloids, and as his wife, estranged though she might have been, she'd had plenty of unwanted attention. Bastian's death had created a lot of fresh interest in her, and she could easily imagine a few new headlines. BASTIAN'S WIDOW LIVING IN POVERTY. BASTIAN'S WIDOW WITHERING AWAY WITH GRIEF. BASTIAN'S WIDOW DISCOVERED ON OBSCURE ISLAND.

'If you are a reporter and you're writing about me, I warn you——'

His eyes narrowed. 'Warn me? Why?'

'I'll sue you!'

'I see,' he said calmly, apparently not impressed by her threat. 'And why would I want to write about you?'

'For money!' she snapped. 'What else?' She turned and marched out of the door, feeling his eyes bore holes in her back and the music weave sensuously around her heart.

'Wait a minute,' he said, his voice quite peremptory, and in spite of all her instincts she stopped and faced him.

'Who are you?' he demanded.

She looked at him squarely. 'Who are *you*?'

'Max Laurello,' he said promptly. He crossed his arms in front of his chest. 'And you?'

'Katrina.'

'Katrina who?'

'It doesn't matter. What is it that you're writing?' An article? An exposé for the gutter Press?'

'A novel.'

'What kind of novel?'

He shrugged. 'Adventure, international intrigue.'

'And I'm in it.'

One eyebrow lifted sardonically. 'No, you are not in it. You merely served as a bit of visual inspiration.'

She wasn't sure if she was angry or insulted or both. A bit of visual inspiration! 'You've certainly mastered the art of giving compliments,' she said caustically.

'It was neither a compliment nor an insult, simply a statement of fact.' He observed her closely as he spoke and his blue gaze made her nervous, which was very annoying. Men didn't often make her nervous.

She glanced at the photographs. Some were rather intriguing—scenes of ferocious-looking men covered in warpaint, dancing; a man, half-dead, crawling through a swamp; a crumbling shack, eerily lit by a full moon; a desert scene containing tents, camels and herdsmen.

She turned away. She'd had enough of this rude, obnoxious male and his sensuous music and his exotic photographs and his supposed novel and his penetrating blue eyes. She wanted to get out, back to the peace and safety of her own house with its many rooms so happily empty of males of any kind. She turned, only to find the way barred by a big woman with a tray in her hand. She wore a flowered dress and had a friendly smile. Smiling was a national pastime on the island of St Barlow. Such sweet relief from big-city hostility! Katrina smiled back and drew aside to let the woman pass.

'Your coffee, sir,' she said and deposited the tray on a table. 'I didn't know you had a visitor. Shall I bring another cup?'

'No, thank you,' said Katrina before Max Laurello could say a thing. 'I'm leaving.'

'You don't have to,' said Max. 'Stay and have some coffee. My concentration is shot to hell as it is, and after all, we are neighbours. No harm in a friendly neighbourly chat, is there?'

A neighbourly chat my foot, she thought. He wasn't getting one iota of information out of her to use as fuel for his book. He'd have to find his inspiration elsewhere; he wasn't going to get it from her if she could help it. She gave him a withering look, which only made him laugh. His anger seemed to have dissipated, but hers hadn't. She liked to hold on to her emotions, savour them and truly experience them.

'I'm busy,' she said, which was a lie, and she was sure he knew it. Turning her back on him, she walked out.

She found her way back home, carefully stepping down the rocky trail. Later that night she lay in bed, hearing in her head the sensuous strains of the violin music, seeing the brilliant blue eyes, seeing the words on the paper as if they were written in her brain:

'Under my hands her skin was smooth as silk.'

She imagined Max's big, tanned hands on her skin, then jerked herself upright in bed, her heart beating wildly.

Something was seriously wrong with her.

On the other hand, maybe something was very right.

She hadn't been interested in men for years. But then she'd been married, of course, and she wasn't *supposed* to be interested in men. She was supposed to be interested in her own husband, which she certainly had been in the beginning. She felt a sudden stab of pain. Oh, how she had loved him! Or thought she had. But the feelings had been difficult to maintain in the face of reality: Bastian hadn't loved her and he'd hardly ever been around. He hadn't been interested in her or their marriage. He'd been interested in other women, and hunting and gambling and various other pleasurable pursuits.

Katrina sighed. It was all so terribly depressing to remember and she didn't want to be depressed. It was all over now. She'd come to the island to restore herself, to gain some weight, to figure out what to do, to learn to smile again and be happy. Doctor's orders, no less.

All she needed was a little magic.

She was lying on her stomach on the beach the next afternoon, engrossed in her book, when a stirring of sand near by diverted her attention. Two large feet came into view, attached to tanned ankles attached to muscular calves. She jerked her head up. Max Laurello loomed large overhead, blue gaze directed downwards. Her pulse leaped crazily. She sat up, dropping her book down in the sand.

'Did you have to sneak up on me like that?' she snapped. 'I could have a heart condition; did you consider that?'

'No,' he said. 'Do you?'

'No.'

'I'm glad to hear that.' He dropped down next to her in the sand, leaning his forearms on his drawn-up knees. He wore khaki shorts and a white polo-shirt. Apparently he had not come to the beach with the idea of taking a swim.

'I'm sorry to disturb you,' he said, 'but——'

'You didn't disturb me, you wrecked my god-damned concentration,' she said promptly.

His left eyebrow quirked up. '*Touché*. I suppose I should apologise.'

'Oh, please, don't strain yourself,' she said, giving him a mock-cheery smile. 'And don't you have anything better to do than laze around on the beach?'

'There's something I'd like to know,' he said, ignoring her barb. 'Why are you so worried that I'm writing about you?'

'I'm not worried.' She gave him a cool smile. 'I was merely warning you.' She grabbed her beach wrap and pulled it on. She was too aware of her bones sticking out. A glimpse of amusement shone in his blue eyes as he watched her and she gave him a stony stare. She kept thinking of the love scene, or at least the beginning of it, that he'd written. She couldn't get it out of her head; it was awful.

He rubbed his chin. 'Your statements make me think that perhaps you are someone in the public eye. If you're rich and famous, why aren't you staying at the Plantation?'

It was not reassuring to know that he had contemplated her belonging to the lofty circles of the famous and the wealthy. Once, of course, she had, but no more. Fortunately she was managing to adjust. She was a flexible, resourceful person. And very, very determined. At least, she tried to think of herself that way.

'I'm insolvent. Broke, in plain English.' Well, relatively speaking.

'I'm familiar with the word,' he said drily. 'Should I know who you are?'

She shrugged. 'Some people do, some people don't. It probably speaks well of you that you don't.' It would mean he didn't read the tabloids.

He scrutinised her some more. 'What is that supposed to mean?'

She waved her hand. 'Nothing, never mind.'

He glanced out over the water. 'So,' he said casually, 'what did you do to become impoverished? Gamble your fortune away?'

'No.' Bastian had managed to do that without her help. She felt, however, no inclination to enlighten Max Laurello.

'What are you going to do about your state of insolvency?' he asked casually.

'I don't know yet.' She traced her finger idly over the gold embossed letters of the book cover. The heroine lay swooning in the hero's arms, her eyes closed, head thrown back.

'Perhaps you ought to find a job,' he suggested helpfully. His eyes lingered meaningfully on the book in her lap and the plastic container of walnut cookies on the towel next to her. All signs of a slothful life.

'An excellent idea,' she agreed. 'I've been considering the various possibilities. They need a brain surgeon at the Mayo clinic, and I was offered a part in a new TV series, but I'm leaning more towards joining a law firm as a partner. I've always thought being a divorce lawyer might be fun. Digging into other people's personal lives—rather exciting, don't you think?'

He ignored this. 'What did you study in college?'

'Child development.' Why was she telling him this?

'Did you want to be a teacher?'

'No.' She clamped her jaws together. She hadn't thought of being a teacher. She'd wanted to be a mother. She'd always wanted to be a mother, ever since she was little. Studying child development had seemed a useful thing to do in preparation for professional motherhood, not to speak of as a way to keep busy while her husband was out gambling and racing cars in alien climes. But here she was, twenty-five years old and no children. Bastian hadn't wanted any. Her hands clenched, grasping sand as she fought an onslaught of emotion. She forced her hands to relax and let the sand slip away between her fingers, aware of the blue gaze intent on her face.

'What are you doing here on the island?' he asked.

'You already know. I'm lazing around on the beach eating chocolates and reading trashy novels.' She took a cookie and defiantly bit into it.

'That's *what* you are doing. But why?'

'I like it.' She smiled sweetly. 'I'm recuperating, actually.' From a case of severe mental exhaustion, she added silently.

He frowned. 'Are you sick?'

'No, I'm not sick,' she said. She selected another cookie.

'How do you stay so thin?' he asked, watching her eat.

She shrugged. 'I'm suffering from a touch of stress. Just run-of-the-mill stuff. Everybody has it.' He cocked a sceptical brow. She smiled sweetly. 'Except you, of course. You gave me such a nice, warm welcome into your home yesterday. No tension there, none at all.'

'I don't like to be disturbed while I'm working.'

She gave him a mocking smile. 'Yeah, I got that idea.'

He looked at her stonily. 'I came to the island to get away from demanding, meddlesome, infuriating females so I could get some work done.'

The man must have a harem. She gave him a sunny smile. 'By all means, don't let me keep you.'

He leaped to his feet and glowered down at her. 'No, I damn well won't.' He turned to make his way back to the path.

'Hey, what did I do?' she called after him. He had come to her, disturbing her peace and quiet, not the other way around.

He turned. 'You're evading my questions.'

She grinned up at him. 'That ought to tell you something about my intellectual prowess.' Did he honestly think she would bare her soul to him, a stranger? A stranger with a computer, no less. A stranger who professed to be a writer.

For a moment he stared at her silently. His face looked vaguely tortured. The man was having a hard time with something and she wasn't sure what or why. He rubbed his forehead. 'It's hot,' he said. 'Come up to my house for a cold drink.'

'No, thank you. I like it hot.' Oh, damn. She hoped he wouldn't take it the wrong way.

His expression did not change. He wasn't taking it any way at all. His mind on more refined matters, the words had not even penetrated his consciousness. 'I need to ask you some questions,' he said.

'I don't do interviews.'

'This is not about you, dammit!'

'Oh? About whom is it, then?'

'About Isabel.' He leaned over, grabbed her hand and pulled her up. 'Are you coming? Or do I carry you?'

CHAPTER TWO

THIS was getting interesting. He wanted to talk about Isabel.

Who was Isabel?

They were standing very close, his blue eyes looking straight into hers, and she could feel her heart begin to pump. His hand was hard and warm and she yanked herself free. He was tall and big and she felt small and vulnerable. Which she was. Five feet two and just under a hundred pounds. He could pick her up and tuck her under his arm and march up the steps to his house with no trouble at all. Movement caught her eye. She glanced up at his house and saw the housekeeper hanging laundry on a washing line. Well, they wouldn't be alone. That at least was reassuring.

She moistened her lips. She noticed the red sparks of fire in his hair, but she refused to be intimidated by him or his hair.

'First you tell me you've come here to escape a harem of women, and now you threaten to drag me up there into your lair. I find it rather confusing.'

He closed his eyes as if praying for strength. 'Why do you women have to make everything so complicated? We're talking about a simple request to come for a drink and a little conversation.'

'It wasn't a request, it was an order. I'm not good at following orders. Besides, I don't know any Isabel.'

'I'll tell you all about her over a long, cold drink.'

'All right, why don't you ask me to come with you nicely? Good manners sometimes work better in getting you what you want.'

He gave her a long-suffering look. 'Would you please come up for a drink? I'd like to talk to you.'

She smiled brightly. 'Thank you, yes, I'd like that.' She didn't have much choice, did she? The best she could do was pretend she did.

So up the rocky path they went to the large veranda of his house and the housekeeper, Mrs Collymore, brought them a large pitcher of soursop juice and two wedges of coconut-cream pie.

Katrina dug in bravely. It was not particularly delicious. Please, she prayed, let it stick to my hips, my ribs, any place.

'Why are you here on the island?' he asked without preamble. 'What attracts you to this isolated kind of life?' It did not sound like an idle question to make idle conversation. It was a question with a purpose.

'Why do you want to know? So you can write some more about me in your book? I thought we were going to discuss Isabel. Who is she? One of your wives or girlfriends you're escaping from?'

He groaned. 'Good God, no. She's a fictitious woman in my book—not you—and she's on this fictitious island——'

'Eating fictitious Belgian chocolates and reading fictitious trashy novels,' she finished for him. 'I know.'

His jaw tightened. 'Yes. And I need to know why she's on the island. Why she's so damned skinny and why she doesn't do anything.'

She leaned back in her chair and observed him. So that was what this was all about. She took a sip from her juice. It was deliciously tart and sweet. 'Make it up. You're the writer. It's all fiction, isn't it?'

He frowned impatiently. 'I've tried making it up. What do you think I've been doing lately?'

'I haven't given it a lot of thought, to tell you the truth. It may surprise you, but you do not feature in my thoughts and dreams.' This was a lie. He had, unfortunately, managed to creep into her dreams and thoughts. Tantalising dreams, embarrassing thoughts. Very annoying, but not to be helped.

A phone began to ring somewhere close by in the room behind them.

'Excuse me,' he said, pushing back his chair and entering the room through the large French windows. The telephone sat on a small side-table just inside the doors.

'Hello?' His voice was curt. A silence followed. Katrina looked out over the dazzling aquamarine sea. A sailing boat floated peacefully through the water beyond the cove.

'Rebecca, for God's sake!' she heard him say impatiently. 'Go ahead and buy it! I gave you the credit card! Use the damned thing!' Another silence. 'I know,' he said then, 'but do you have to call me for every little thing?'

Silence again. She was sitting here listening to his telephone conversation to a certain Rebecca and there was nothing she could do about it save get up and walk off the veranda.

'Not for a while,' came his voice. 'I'm having trouble with the damned book. Believe me, you're better off without me.'

Katrina bit her lip. She could believe that. Anybody, any time, would be better off without him. He was rude, impatient, overbearing and self-centred. It had taken no time at all to come to that diagnosis. Too bad he was so good-looking. Those blue eyes were really something. They could wreak devastation in someone's heart. Well, as long as it wasn't hers. She'd already had her share of devastation. She felt an unexpected pang of pain and she clamped her jaws together.

A moment later Max was back on the veranda, easing his tall frame into the creaky rattan chair, his blue gaze back on her face.

'Where were we?'

'Something about your not being able to come up with a reason why this woman in your book came to the island.'

'Right, yes. Have you heard of writer's block?'

She nodded. 'Vaguely. Something about all the taps of imagination turning off, the inspiration drying up, the creativity shrivelling away and the mind going crazy,' she said theatrically. 'For weeks and weeks and months and months,' she added unmercifully. 'Something like that? Is that what makes you so wild and crazy and rude?'

He gave her a stony stare. 'You've got it.' He was not amused, she could tell.

'That's not what it looked like when I saw you yesterday. You were writing away like a man possessed. You were even accusing me of having wrecked your precious concentration.'

'My block is only partial. It relates solely to the woman.'

'Skinny Isabel.'

He nodded, picked up his glass and drained it.

'Well, why don't I help you out?' she said generously. She sat back and stared up into the greenery of the big-leaved almond tree shading the veranda. 'Perhaps she came to the island to recuperate from a trauma. Say she found out that her husband is sleeping around with another woman and now she's trying to make up her mind whether to divorce him or not.'

He gave her a narrow-eyed look. 'Is he?'

'Is who what?'

'Is your husband sleeping around and do you want to divorce him?'

She laughed. 'You do underestimate my intelligence, don't you?'

'Just answer the damned question!'

She gave him a hard, silent stare.

'Please,' he added pseudo-politely.

She contemplated his question for a moment. 'I don't have a husband,' she said then.

'Divorced?'

'No.'

He gave her a long, assessing look, obviously contemplating his next query. She wasn't going to give him the opportunity.

'We were talking about Isabel,' she reminded him, 'not me.'

He frowned. 'Yes, right.'

'I was suggesting that her husband might be cheating on her and she's——'

'No,' he said, interrupting her. 'I don't like the thing about men fooling around. It's too commonplace. Think of something else. Another reason, something more dramatic.'

Men fooling around. So heart-wrenching. So devastating. Yet so commonplace. So commonplace, he was probably doing it himself. Her body tensed involuntarily and she felt a stab of anger. Damn you, Bastian, she thought. Damn all you philandering men. She stared out over the crystalline sea and gathered her composure.

'All right, how about this? Maybe her whole family got wiped out in a tornado and she's the only one left and her house is a pile of rubble and——'

'No.' He waved his hand impatiently.

'She's a Hollywood star and her career is down the drain due to vicious gossip——'

'No.' He raked his hand through his hair. 'This is not going to work.'

'It might help if I knew something about Isabel. Is she nice, smart, stupid, mean? What role is she supposed to play in this book? Is she a spy? A schoolteacher? A famous singer?'

He was silent for a moment. 'I'm not sure,' he said finally. 'That's the problem. She's not really there yet in my mind. I can't quite get a grasp on her character.'

'When in doubt, throw it out. Maybe she doesn't belong. Get rid of her. No car wreck, though, it's so unimaginative. Let her jump off a cliff or something.'

He glowered at her as if she'd committed a mortal sin. 'No, I can't do that. I need her.'

'What for?'

'Isabel is the woman who brings my hero back to life, emotionally speaking. He doesn't have a favourable opinion about women, but Isabel is different.'

'Different how?'

'I don't know!' He stood up and began to pace restlessly along the veranda, hands in his shorts pockets. 'My problem is I have no experience with women being different.'

'Different from what?'

He glared at her. 'Never mind.'

'A-ha,' she said meaningfully. 'Another casualty in the war between the male and female of the species. Is that why you came to the island? To lick your wounds?'

His expression was not encouraging. She came to her feet. 'I think I'll leave,' she announced. 'I have the feeling I'm not adding anything to the creative process here.'

She went down the veranda steps, not waiting for a reply. When she looked up from the path, she saw him watching her, his face dark and brooding. She hesitated for a moment, then leaped back up the creaky wooden stairs.

'I think what you ought to try every day for a week is some fresh grated onion in a glass of warm milk with some honey. It would do wonders for your disposition.'

She drove to St Mary's Orphanage that afternoon, cruising along the narrow curving coastal road in her sky-blue Mini Moke. It was a boxy little vehicle with a canvas roof and no sides and she loved the feel of the tradewind breeze in her face. It would be nice to feel it in her hair if she had any, but very short hair was not impressed by a little wind.

Two years ago she'd visited the famous Giovanni Hair Studios in Rome. She'd been looking for a 'new look' and she had received it: she had lost almost all her hair, a long length of heavy silk that had reached well down her back. Giovanni had persuaded her that nothing should detract from her marvellous bone-structure, the exquisite shape of her skull and the regal line of her throat. He had gone positively lyrical, lapsing from his accented English into poetic Italian. Dancing around her chair with excitement, gesturing with enthusiasm, he'd showered praise as if she were a veritable sculpture. It had never occurred to her that her skull and facial bone-structure could be considered a piece of art, as so obviously Giovanni did. Off with the hair, demanded Giovanni, and who was she to refuse the famous Italian hair stylist, the great artist in the hair department? She hadn't had it in her. So off had come the hair.

After the deed was done, she had looked at herself in amazement. Who was this beautiful creature? Her eyes had looked twice as large, her mouth twice as full. There was the delicate curve of chin and cheek and throat. She was, it seemed, a different person.

Not that it had changed anything in her life. Her husband had kept on hunting and gambling and she had been just as lonely as before, her studies and a busy social life notwithstanding.

But the sea breeze felt good on her face, if not in her hair, and she smiled at nothing in particular because she felt quite happy today, quite alive and energised as she cruised along the coastal road towards St Mary's Orphanage.

St Mary's was located in a restored sugar mill just outside Ginger Bay, a tiny fishing village not far from her villa. At the moment it was home to nine abandoned babies and children—healthy new-borns, handicapped toddlers, and malnourished children. Katrina went to the orphanage several times a week to play with the children and read them stories.

She was welcomed, as always, with smiles and cheers. The children came rushing up to her, hung on her arms, clamped themselves around her legs and danced around her. Obviously she was not wrecking anybody's concentration here. It was a comforting thought. Within minutes, as always, Sister Angelica produced a cup of tea for her, adulterated with powder milk and five spoons of sugar. It was a sickly-sweet brew and the only reason Katrina drank it was the hopeful vision of all those calories racing to her hips, happily settling in and staying put.

As she sat down with her tea, Sasha Grant arrived, bringing fresh goat's milk for the children. Sasha was a gorgeous, tall redhead with green eyes and a laughing mouth.

'Hi!' she greeted Katrina, as she put the milk containers on the kitchen counter. 'I was going to call you. I have a new kind of cheese I thought you might like to try.'

She sat down at the table and Sister Bernadette rushed to pour her a cup of tea as well, minus the milk and sugar, which Sasha abhorred.

Sasha's husband was the doctor who ran the island's small teaching hospital which took care of the children's medical needs for free. Apart from being beautiful, Sasha was smart and had a talent for business. When she had come to the island she had started a small goat dairy, producing goat's butter and various kinds of goat's cheese which she sold all over the Caribbean to fancy hotels and restaurants. Katrina, being a lover of cheese of all kinds, stopped by regularly to see what was new on the cheese front.

'I'd love to try it,' she said to Sasha. 'I'll stop by on my way back home. What kind is it?'

So they talked cheese until the tea was finished and it was time for Sasha to return to the dairy to tend to her goats and for Katrina to go to the playroom to tend to the children.

She sat on the floor, children snuggled on her lap and cuddled by her side, and read them stories. The children made her smile. They were happy to have her there, to take from her whatever love and care she had to offer. I have plenty, she thought, feeling her heart flow over as she looked at the small, trusting faces, felt the small, warm bodies nestling against her own. It was a good feeling to be so wanted.

She hadn't felt wanted and needed for a very long time.

She made lists. Lists of things to do, books to read, people to call, decisions to make, letters to write.

She loved lists. They made her feel organised. They made her feel she was *doing* something.

It was almost five and Katrina sat on the veranda updating her lists. There were two more lists to make, two lists she had put off for a quite a while. However, the time had come to make these lists. She sighed and took a fresh piece of paper. She stared at the blank sheet, pen poised. This was not going to be easy. She took a deep breath.

'TALENTS, SKILLS AND ACCOMPLISHMENTS', she wrote at the top of the page. Then her mind went blank. It was terrifying. Surely she, Katrina MacKenzie, née Sinclair, was not merely a skinny body with nothing inside? A vacuum. An empty lot. She, who wasn't even a gorgeous blonde!

She closed her eyes. Why was this so difficult? She was so very well educated. She could distinguish Bach from Beethoven, a Rembrandt from a Renoir, a Dior original from an Yves St Laurent, a Mercedes from a Maserati. She knew the finest restaurants in New York, Rome, Paris, Sydney, Rio, Singapore and other choice locations around the world. She could say 'hello', 'thank you' and 'where is the ladies' room?' in a dozen languages, Swahili and Malay among them. It was distressing that none of this knowledge could be recycled into profitable employment. Even her degree in child development wasn't enough for a good career. She'd need at least another two years and a more advanced degree.

She chewed on the end of her gold Parker pen and concentrated hard. What she needed were marketable talents and skills, the operative word being marketable. Her eyes caught the French cookbook on the rattan coffee-table and suddenly a light came on in her head. She began to write.

1) Cook gourmet food
2) Grow herbs and medicinal plants
3)

Her pen hovered helplessly next to the number three, her mind once more drawing a blank. Two items. It was pathetic. Surely there was something more she could do?

She could entertain, put on dinners and parties. All right. She filled it in behind the 3.

A list of three items. It was depressing. Long lists were so much more satisfying.

She took another sheet of paper. 'JOB AND CAREER POSSIBILITIES', she wrote. The thought was nerve-racking. She stared at the paper. Then, bravely, she began to write.

1) Grow fresh herbs for restaurants or gourmet shops
2) Start a catering business in New York
3) Write cookbooks
4) Make and sell herbal medicines or cosmetics, et cetera.

There! Who said she had nothing to offer society? There were always possibilities to make yourself useful. All you had to do was really concentrate and dig deep inside to find hidden talents and possibilities.

She felt much better. What she needed to do was research the various options, take stock of her resources and make a decision.

She jumped up from her chair, danced around the table and laughed out loud. She felt great!

Several busy days later, at exactly twelve o'clock noon, Katrina was overcome with a craving for some true, authentic island food. This happened now and then. Fortunately, it was a craving easily indulged. Not far down the road was a food stall shaded by a huge banyan tree which offered deliciously greasy conch fritters, loaded with calories. Conch were edible creatures which lived in sea-shells, and made into fritters they were un-recognisable and delectable. The stall's vendor, Josephine, was an enormous black lady with a flowered dress, a straw hat, and the gift of the gab. She knew all the island gossip and entertained her customers with the latest scandals, rumours, and joyful happenings. Josephine had a reputation for being knowledgeable and wise, and many people sought her out for advice in matters of love and family life.

Katrina strolled down the road, trying hard to keep her pace down. She did not want to expend more calories than absolutely necessary. She wanted to hang on to as many as she could, but it wasn't easy. It was more in her nature to keep a steady pace and swing her arms and skip a little here and there, for it was a wonderful day. There were many wonderful days on St Barlow. Maybe she should consider living here permanently.

Live permanently on St Barlow? She stopped walking and stared absently at the ginger thomas bushes by the road as she digested the thought. A hummingbird fluttered frantically among the bell-shaped yellow flowers, searching for just the perfect bloom.

Maybe she could grow herbs here and sell them to the Plantation and to the other resorts and luxury hotels in the Caribbean. They could be flown in fresh every few days. She could also make herbal medicines here, study the preparations traditional to the islands, perhaps market them to speciality shops in the States.

She raised her arms above her head, up to the blue, blue sky, and laughed out loud, skipping. What an idea!

She walked around the bend in the road and her good spirits sank with a crash. There was Max, sitting on the wooden bench at Josephine's stall, eating conch fritters.

It wasn't fair!

'Well, hello there,' he greeted her. He sounded quite civilised. He looked relaxed, but his face with its prominent nose and square jaw had not lost any of its arrogance. The bright blue eyes were observing her intently. She found it quite unnerving and all her instincts told her to turn and run. She didn't. She merely stood there and stared at him, feeling every inch of her react to him as if he held some magnetic power over her.

Not a comforting thought. In fact, it was terrifying.

Josephine smiled broadly and urged her to take a seat. Her English had a lilting Caribbean flavour and was a joy to the ear. She was just frying up a fresh batch of fritters, she said, and she had some very interesting news.

'Actually, I was only taking a walk,' Katrina lied. 'I already had lunch.'

'You could use some more,' stated Max. 'Sit.'

She sat. The smell of the fritters was much too seductive. Well, that was what she told herself. Also, her heart was beating a little fast suddenly and it needed a rest.

Josephine put a cold bottle of sorrel soda in front of her. It was what she always had with her fritters. She took a long drink. It was cool and delicious.

'I want to ask you a question,' said Max, taking a swig from his beer.

'Oh, please, not again,' she moaned, shifting away from him a little. He was sitting too close. She could see the individual dark hairs on his arm and hand. A brown, muscular arm, a big, strong hand with long fingers and square nails. She liked good hands on a man. Strong hands, gentle fingers. Oh, God, what was she thinking?

'What the hell was that revolting thing about onion and milk and honey?' he asked.

She laughed. It sounded a little breathless. 'Just a folk remedy. Helps to purify the digestive tract, which is good for a general sense of well-being and happiness.'

One brow lifted derisively. 'So why are you concerned with my well-being and happiness?'

She wished her heart would calm its crazy rhythm. She smiled cheerfully. 'It was merely a bit of friendly, neighbourly advice. You're rather morose and bad-tempered, aren't you?'

'I have hardly slept in weeks.'

'I know how that feels,' she commiserated, remembering lawyers and accountants terrorising her days and haunting her nights. 'I have some wonderful stuff, though. *Schlaf wohl Tropfen*. Got it in Switzerland.'

'Spare me,' he said.

'It's a mixture of lemon balm, hops and oat juice,' she went on, unperturbed. 'Works like a charm. At least, for me it did.'

One corner of his mouth tipped upwards. 'Are you a witch doctor or something?'

'Witchery has nothing to do with it. It's pure science.' She took the plate Josephine offered her and bit into a hot conch fritter. 'Mmm. Delicious.'

Josephine had stories to tell and she was determined they shouldn't miss a thing.

For half an hour they listened to her mellow Caribbean voice and didn't miss a thing. It was riveting. So riveting, in fact, that Katrina almost forgot that she was sitting next to the disagreeable Max Laurello, author of adventure novels.

Almost, but not quite. She was enthralled by Josephine's tales, but on a different, deeper level she was acutely aware of Max—his body, his movements, the way his fingers held the pencil as he was taking notes in a small notebook he'd extracted from his pocket. It seemed that Josephine's island sagas were very inspirational.

Another customer arrived and Josephine's attention was diverted. Max put his notebook away.

Katrina took a drink from her sorrel soda. 'I wonder if I could borrow one of your books?' she said to Max. 'One that you've written.' It might prove to be revealing.

'No,' he said.

She stared at him, surprised. 'Why not?'

'I don't have any with me here.'

She sighed. 'I've got nothing left to read. It makes me very edgy. 'You have something else I could borrow?'

'No,' he said again. He finished the last of his beer and pushed the bottle away from him.

This was too crazy. 'You mean to say you have no books in your house? Nothing? Not even a horror novel or a whodunit?' She looked at his mouth. A very manly mouth, strong but sensual. Very disturbing. She moved her gaze upwards to his eyes. Everything about him was disturbing.

He grimaced. 'You like horror?'

His question made her smile. 'No. I was thinking of what *you* might like. Horror, I would guess, psycho-thrillers, or something with lots of blood and gore.'

He glowered at her, then glanced back at the fresh fritter Josephine had slid on to his plate. 'I don't have your kind of books,' he said sanctimoniously, and bit into the fritter.

'You have no idea what kind of books I read.' His presumption was quite infuriating.

He gave her a sceptical look. No doubt he was re-membering the book she'd been reading on the beach, the book whose titillating cover he had been able to ob-serve closely.

'Tell me,' he said with exaggerated patience, 'what kind of books do you read?'

'I'm a very eclectic reader,' she said loftily. 'I read almost anything but blood and gore—historical novels, science fiction, mystery. But what I like most of all is fantasy.'

His left eyebrow quirked briefly. 'Fantasy?'

'Yes. Fairy-tales for grown-ups. Mysterious kingdoms, ancient prophecies, magic powers, wizards and quests and adventures and all that good stuff.'

He grew very still. He forgot to chew. An odd, far-away look came into his eyes. Then he swallowed and his bright blue gaze focused on her face again, intent, disquieting.

'Why? Why do you like fantasy?'

She thought for a moment. 'Because anything is possible.' In her own fairy-tale fantasy she had a loving husband and a house full of children. In your dreams anything was possible, even magic.

'Because anything is possible,' he repeated slowly. 'I like that.' He smiled suddenly, and it was quite a wondrous sight to see his scowling, morose expression turn into something so bright and sunny and quite...sexy. Her heart made a little leap of excitement and she couldn't help but smile back at him.

He jumped to his feet, fished some money out of his pocket and slapped it on the rough wooden table. The next moment he was off, striding down the road in the direction of his house as if pursued by a pack of wolves.

'He be in a big hurry,' said Josephine and laughed. She counted out the money. 'Dis plenty for two,' she said. 'I tink he pay for you.'

'I'm paying for myself, thank you,' said Katrina, digging for money in her shorts pocket.

'Why?' Josephine's sharp eyes observed her keenly.

'Because,' said Katrina succinctly.

Josephine shrugged and held out her hand. 'OK, I take it.' Josephine knew a business opportunity when she saw it.

As she walked home, Katrina realised that she still did not have anything to read.

She took her time cooking her own dinner that evening, perfecting a recipe of her own creation: grilled wild rabbit with mango purée. She had just put the food on the table when the front doorbell rang.

She went to the door, which opened directly into the large, tiled sitting-room, and wondered who would arrive so ceremoniously by the front door, rather than come up the stairs to the veranda.

The person who was Max, with a box of books. Her heart lurched at the sight of him. He wore lightweight trousers and an open-necked shirt with a rather exotic island print. His tall frame filled up the doorway.

'I thought you didn't have any books,' she said, willing her heart to calm down.

'I found some.' He gave a crooked smile. 'My conscience got the better of me. Not having anything to read is a terrible thing.'

'You tell me.'

He sniffed. 'What smells so good?'

'I'm cooking dinner.' He looked hungry. She remembered it was his cook's day off, a bit of information she'd obtained from him over conch fritters at lunchtime. Her eyes settled on the box of books—a veritable treasure of pleasure. One good deed deserved another, did it not? She struggled briefly with her conscience.

'You're welcome to stay,' she said bravely. 'I have plenty for two.'

His eyes met hers and he smiled. 'I'd be delighted,' he said, sounding like a perfect gentleman. Was he trying to confuse her?

'Come on in,' she invited, and put the books down on a small table, fighting the impulse to sit down right then and there and examine the titles.

Max looked around the spacious, high-ceilinged sitting-room, his glance taking in the rattan furniture, the big flowered cushions on the floor, the bright paintings by a local artist on the walls, the large tropical plants everywhere. One side of the room was left open to the columned veranda, cabana style—no doors, no windows. There was no crime on St Barlow; there wasn't even a prison.

'Quite a house, this,' he said.

'Yes. A little big for only one person, but great for giving parties and having house guests.'

'Of which I have seen none,' he stated.

'True,' she admitted. She'd wanted to be alone.

'Are you renting it or is it yours?'

'It's mine.'

'But you don't live here permanently, I take it?'

'I live in New York, mostly.' At least she'd used to. There wasn't any place to go home to now.

'Are you a fashion model, by any chance?' Max asked.

A model. Well, she did have that starving look, didn't she? She laughed. 'No. I'm five feet two. They want them tall.'

'You walk as if you are.'

'And how is that?' His eyes were so intense, they made her nervous.

His mouth curved. 'You've got that ... how shall I say this? You've got that confident, go-to-hell kind of walk.'

'It's all a show. I'm actually very shy and insecure.'

He laughed. 'Yes, I noticed.'

She glowered at him. 'You don't know what's in my soul.'

'So enlighten me.'

'You wish. The next thing I know it'll be in your book.'

He gave a crooked grin. 'You don't trust me, do you?'

'Not for a minute.' She produced a sunny smile. 'Well, let's eat before the food gets cold.'

The dining-room too was open to the sitting-room, just around the corner. He followed her, staring at the table with surprise.

It was set with a white and pink tablecloth and a lush arrangement of tropical flowers. Two pink candles in crystal candlesticks bathed the scene in a soft, romantic glow. The grilled rabbit, arranged beautifully on a white platter, looked delicious.

'Are you expecting someone?'

'No. See, the table is only set for one.' Quickly she set another place across from hers. If only she could make it through dinner. She'd been crazy to invite him in. This big man was overpowering the room, charging the atmosphere. Every cell of her body was standing to attention.

He gave her an incredulous look. 'You do this for yourself?'

'Yes. It's part of a survival strategy for people living alone: Treat yourself as if you were a treasured guest.'

He laughed out loud, a good, honest laugh, and she liked the sound of it. Then he held out her chair for her and she sat down. He lowered himself on to the chair across from her and offered to pour the wine. There was a silence as he did so and she found it nerve-racking. It was absurd. What was the matter with her?

Max ate with great appetite. 'This is gourmet fare,' he said. 'It's delicious.'

A compliment! Her heart made a joyful little dance. Silly maybe, but she so enjoyed a compliment now and then, but then everybody did. Compliments were vitamins for the ego, weren't they? And, she had to admit, compliments from Max Laurello seemed extra-potent. 'Thank you,' she said nicely.

His eyes narrowed a little as he observed her, curiosity and a faint incredulity on his face. 'Where did you learn to cook like this?'

She made a casual gesture. 'Oh, here and there.' Paris, Rome, New York. She felt an odd tension in her body and every time he looked at her a teasing, tingling sensation shivered through her. Damn, it was annoying. She took another drink of wine, hoping for strength and composure during this most awkward situation. What if he noticed?

'I'd expected you to be strictly a convenience-food eater if someone didn't cook for you,' he commented.

'Not on your life. I like real food. Fresh food. The way it comes out of the ground or grows on trees. Mother Nature does a better job than anybody.'

He stared at his plate, a far-away look in his eyes.

'Why don't you make Isabel a vegetarian?' she suggested.

He looked up, frowning. 'What makes you say that?'

'Because you were thinking about her and how to develop her and it was just an idea that came into my head. It's called inspiration, I think.'

'You're not a vegetarian,' he observed, glancing at the meat on his plate.

'What does that have to do with anything?' She knew what. Isabel was being modelled after her, Katrina the skinny.

He shrugged. 'Merely making an observation.'

They had small guava tarts for dessert, which he duly praised. They were, indeed, very pretty and delicious. She liked food to look beautiful. They took their coffee to the veranda, which was lit by small lamps and large candles. It seemed oddly intimate to sit here with him in the balmy night air, looking out over the tranquil sea glimmering seductively in the moonlight. The air was filled with the perfumy scent of night-blooming jasmine, and the velvet sky was studded with stars. It was all so perfectly romantic, it was maddening.

A box of children's books sat on the floor by her chair, sent to her by Mary Lou, her best friend in New York, for the children of St Mary's orphanage.

Max picked up some of the books and examined them with consternation on his face. '*Winnie the Pooh*? *Stormy with a Chance of Meatballs*? *Charlie and the Chocolate Factory*?'

'You read very well,' she said drily.

'What are these?' he asked.

'Children's books. See, they have pictures and big letters.'

'Don't tell me you read children's books, too.'

'Yes, I do, actually. Some of them are wonderful. Life lessons to be learned. You should read them some time.'

He gave her a long, silent look. She bit her lip, suppressing a laugh. 'I go to the orphanage twice a week and read to the kids there,' she confessed. 'They needed some new books, so I asked my friend Mary Lou to send me some.'

'The orphanage?' he asked. 'The one run by the nuns? The one in that restored sugar mill?'

'Yes.'

He nodded and a distant look came into his blue eyes. Katrina gave a deep sigh of resignation. 'I think reading to cute little orphans would be a lovely thing for Isabel to be doing. I'm sure she has a very well-developed sense of social duty, her saving the hero and all.'

He glanced at her, but he wasn't really hearing her words. His mind was far off in his fictitious world with his fictitious woman, skinny Isabel, who read stories to fictitious children in a fictitious orphanage, no doubt.

He drank his coffee absently. She wanted to hit him over the head with *Winnie the Pooh*. She managed, however, to control herself. It was one of the things she had learned to do, being well-brought-up.

The coffee finished, he stood up to leave. He seemed in a hurry to go home. It wasn't hard to think why. Irresistible Isabel called. Mechanically offering his thanks for the lovely dinner, he was off, down the stairs, at record speed.

'I should have hit him over the head after all,' she said out loud to herself.

Well, why did she care? She'd wanted him to leave, hadn't she? The man was getting on her nerves and she didn't like it. She didn't relish the idea of him having such an impact on her nervous system.

Later, as she casually looked out of her bedroom window—well, maybe it wasn't so casual—she could see the light on in his office. He'd be up with Isabel half the night, or maybe even the whole night.

'I hate you, Isabel,' she muttered, surprising herself. Now why had she said a stupid thing like that?

CHAPTER THREE

KATRINA didn't see Max for several days. It was so peaceful! So relaxing! Then one morning he came leaping up the stairs to the veranda where she was consulting a new list—'CONTACTS TO CONTACT'—listing all the people who might help her with information on the various career possibilities she had on her 'JOBS AND CAREER POSSIBILITIES' list. She'd made many calls in the last few days and her new sense of purpose made her feel good. Many questions loomed. What types of cookbooks were presently popular? Was there a market for fresh herbs at Caribbean restaurants? And so forth. The idea of settling on the island was still very tempting, but it seemed prudent to explore all her options before making a final decision.

'When are you going to St Mary's again?' Max asked. He hadn't even said hello. He did not always seem quite conscious of the here and now and the civilities required of life in the real world. He stood in the sunlight, hair glinting, and he looked big and powerful and very sexy dressed casually in white shorts and a blue T-shirt that matched his eyes.

'Good morning to you too,' she said, feeling her body tense.

He frowned. 'Good morning. Didn't I say that?'

'No, you didn't. Your mind was occupied otherwise and you couldn't quite manage it. You asked me when I was going to St Mary's again.'

'When are you?'

'Why do you want to know?'

'I want to go with you.'

She laughed. 'You do, do you?'

'I want to observe you while you read to the kids. Take some pictures.'

'No way.'

He frowned, raking his hand through his hair. Red sparked dangerously. 'For heaven's sake, what's the big deal?'

.'I don't like my pictures in the tabloids.'

He muttered a curse. 'If I wanted a picture of you for the tabloids, do you think I would ask? Do you think I'd want one of you reading to orphaned children? Good God, woman, use your head! If I'd wanted to, I could have sold dozens of photos of you by now. Shots of you lying on the beach in your bikini, for instance.'

How true. She wondered if he'd found out who she was.

'I do *not* write for the tabloids,' he went on. 'Stop being so damned paranoid.' He crossed his arms in front of his chest and regarded her impatiently. 'Now, how about it?'

'You don't just come barging into some private place and take pictures of people.'

'I'll ask permission from whomever is in charge over there, and I'm asking you now if you'd be so kind as to let me photograph you while you read to the children.'

'Why?' As if she didn't know.

He rolled his eyes heavenwards. 'Because I need them to look at for my writing.'

'Ah, yes, I remember now. Visual inspiration.'

His eyes held hers for a silent moment. 'I'm not writing about you, I promise.'

'You're writing about Isabel, I know.' Why did she feel as if she was being used? Because she was, of course.

He raked his hands through his hair and sighed irritably. 'I didn't think this was such an indiscreet request. It's not as if I'm asking you to pose in the nude, for God's sake.'

She gave him a frigid stare, remaining eloquently silent. A wolfish look came into his eyes. 'Of course, if that would appeal to you more, I would consider——'

'Drop dead,' she said succinctly, and he laughed.

'All right, forget that idea. Let me go to the orphanage with you.'

Had anyone else asked her, she wouldn't have minded at all. It was the fact that it was Max wanting to take photos. For his book.

'I don't know you, or what kind of book you're writing. I don't know that I want anything to do with it.'

'Adventure, international intrigue. I told you. No blood and gore of significance. Just a couple of clean killings, that's all. You can read it when it's finished. You can sue me if you want.'

How generous he was! 'How many books have you written?'

'This is my fifth.'

'All published?'

'Yes. The fourth is coming out next month.'

'Why don't I know your name?'

He shrugged. 'There are thousands of writers and thousands of books out there. You can't know them all.'

There was no arguing with that logic. 'Why don't you have any of your own books with you?'

'What is this? An interrogation?'

'Yes. Why don't you have any of your own books?'

He glanced heavenwards in exasperation. 'I don't carry my books around with me. Besides, I left Vermont in a hurry.'

'Vermont? Is that where you're from?'

'Yes, and let's not digress. May I please take some photos of you reading to the kids?'

She felt a sudden, delicious sense of power. He wanted something from her, and she had the power to refuse. It wouldn't be very nice if she did, of course. In fact, it would be childish. And she, Katrina, was not a childish person.

So let him take the pictures, she said to herself. She didn't have the energy to make a big deal out of something insignificant. She had the ominous feeling that she needed to save her energy for more important matters, whatever they might turn out to be.

'All right, then,' she relented. 'As long as you have Sister Bernadette's permission, and as long as you give me and them copies. They'd like that.'

'No problem.'

'And as long as what you are writing is pure fiction.'

He put his hand over his heart. 'Boy Scout's honour.'

'Otherwise I will sue you.'

'Understood.'

'And I have contacts,' she said darkly. 'I will win.'

'You sound dangerous,' he said, giving her a mildly mocking look.

'I am. You'd better believe it.' She held his blue gaze. It was so very blue. She swallowed with great difficulty. 'I'll be reading to the kids again Friday morning.'

'Thank you. I appreciate it.' He smiled into her eyes, and her heart lurched. It really was a nice smile. So charming, so sexy.

So very dangerous.

He was quite a photographer. Very professional. She couldn't help but be impressed by the way he moved around, snapping pictures from various angles, manoeuvring his limbs with the easy grace of long practice. Her gaze seemed fixed to his body as she watched him work.

The children were still having their mid-morning snack and were fascinated by him and his camera. The nuns, too, were enjoying themselves. He'd done quite a job charming them and one of them had rushed around bringing him a cup of tea with milk and a ton of sugar, which he bravely downed.

Snack time over, the children gathered around her in the shade of the big mango tree. Max joked with them and made them laugh, then he gently instructed them to listen to the story and tried to make himself as inconspicuous as possible. Soon they forgot about him, engrossed in the story she read them, no longer distracted by the click of the camera.

'I owe you lunch,' said Max when the reading session was over. 'Shall we drive into Port Royal and find something there?'

It was difficult to refuse such a gentlemanly offer, so she decided not to fight it.

'I'd like that.' She was feeling, at the moment at least, rather mellow towards him. Watching him interact with the children had done that. It was difficult to harbour negative feelings towards a man who displayed such a natural way with children. It wasn't what she had expected; this man seemed to have a surprising array of sides to his character.

He had a red Mini Moke, Mini Mokes being the national car of St Barlow. Katrina sat back and savoured the feel of the wind in her face, enjoying the lovely scenery as they drove towards the capital. The road was narrow, weaving through small villages with pastel-coloured houses, fields of green sugar cane and groves of rustling coconut palms. On her right massive volcanic mountains, lush with green rainforest, reared up to the blue sky. Secrets were hidden there in the damp, green darkness of the forest—plants and trees with healing powers. Green magic. It was a very exciting thought.

'Do you spend much time here on the island?' Max asked.

'Once or twice a year for a couple of weeks. Longer this time.' Sometimes she would come alone, just to get away. Other times Bastian had wanted her here if he'd decided to come to the island with a group of friends to go scuba-diving or sailing. He'd needed her to be hostess.

'What do you do in New York?' he asked.

'I was in college until a couple of years ago and after that I travelled and studied in Europe. Cooking courses, things like that.' And skiing in Switzerland and visiting friends in Rio and Hong Kong and trying not to think about what her husband might be doing. Trying very hard, but not always succeeding.

They passed a farmer with a donkey loaded high with bananas. The farmer smiled, waving his machete in greeting, and they waved back.

'Why did you leave Vermont in a hurry?' She was anxious to change the focus of the conversation.

He looked puzzled.

'That's what you told me a couple of days ago. Did you run away from the police or something?'

'Worse,' he said.

'The FBI?'

'Women,' he said.

Women. Plural. Well, she was not impressed.

He cursed under his breath and braked hard to avoid hitting a pregnant goat that came strolling across the road. 'See, females of any sort get in my way,' he said.

'My heart bleeds for you. What kind of aftershave do you use? Musk?'

'Can't you tell?'

'No, I'm immune.'

'Oh, I see.' He grinned. 'Now that sounds like a challenge if ever I heard one.'

'Only you are not interested. You came to the island to avoid women, remember?'

'True. Well, then we're both lucky. I don't have to worry about you and you don't have to worry about me.'

'Perfect,' she said brightly. So what were the two of them doing in the same car, on the way to have some lunch together? Business, that was what. A simple courtesy business lunch. Very civilised. So why wouldn't her heart relax?

They had lunch at the Sugar Bay Inn, where a buffet table offered them deep-fried flying fish, goat curry, pickled breadfruit, cornmeal-coconut bread, fried plantain and other Caribbean delicacies.

The Sugar Bay Inn was the only hotel and restaurant of any significance in Port Royal, a remnant of colonial days full of faded splendour—antique furniture, threadbare red carpeting, the faint smell of old wood and wax. The old-time ambience of the place was wonderful.

They had a table by the window, overlooking the harbour where yachts, fishing boats and cargo ships bobbed gently in the water.

'You love children, don't you?' asked Max out of the blue.

She looked up from her plate, surprised. 'Yes, why do you ask?'

He shrugged. 'It was very obvious, the way you were playing with them. You're a natural. I think I got some good shots.'

They talked about the orphanage and the children, which she was happy to do, and about the island and the wonders of hiking in the rainforest, on the mountains, and a restaurant they both knew in New York. A very companionable, easy conversation it was. On the surface. It would have been better yet if he hadn't had such nice hands. She kept looking at them as he ate. And his eyes! Why did they have to be so blue? Why did they have to look at her with this intensity, this keen interest? It was really quite disturbing at times. Her heart never quite relaxed its rhythm and an odd tension seemed to invade her body whenever he was near. No man had ever had such an impact on her.

They skipped dessert, but lingered over their coffee, a strong island brew that was delicious and hopefully would keep her alert during the rest of the afternoon. She had work to do. She had to plan for the future and make phone calls. She had a list: 'PHONE CALLS TO MAKE'.

They drove back, past fields of pineapple and banana bushes, past the ancient little church, the Ark of Love Catholic church, back through the fishing village of Ginger Bay. Emmaline, who owned the village general store, waved at them. The store was painted pale violet and had bright turquoise shutters. In front, baskets full of papaya, tomatoes, mangoes and other produce made a colourful display.

Out of Ginger Bay, the road led past the sea, giving peaceful vistas of the glittering aquamarine waters and powdery white beaches. It was all so idyllic, so utterly serene.

'Paradise,' Max stated, as if he had guessed her thoughts. He made an expansive gesture, indicating the island, the exotic scenery, the azure sky overhead. 'So much peace and quiet.'

A wing-flapping chicken ran squawking across the road in front of them, narrowly missing death, and flung itself hysterically into the bushes. Katrina laughed.

'I thought Vermont was peaceful and quiet,' she said.

He grimaced. 'It would be, without women.'

'You seem to have this hang-up about women. So what am I? Did you not actually invite me into your car, to go out and have lunch, no less? Do I take this as an act of great bravery on your part?'

A bemused expression darkened the blue of his eyes. 'You're different,' he said mysteriously.

Well, she hoped so. The idea of being like everyone else, a sheep among sheep, was terrifying. She'd rather think of herself as a woman unique. Apparently he seemed to think of women as a group of identical individuals, out to get him *en masse*. But she, Katrina, was different. She wondered how he saw her.

'How am I different?' she asked.

He stared straight ahead at the road, his expression unreadable, and for the longest time he said nothing. Then he gave her a quick, sideways glance, his blue gaze meeting hers. 'I don't know,' he said in a low voice, 'but I intend to find out.'

She felt a deep thrill of excitement; she couldn't help it. The sound of his voice, the look in his eyes sparked something deep inside her.

She was a woman of mystery. So he seemed to think. She'd never thought of herself as mysterious, but it certainly sounded fascinating. She, Katrina MacKenzie, was a mysterious, fascinating woman. How exciting!

'Mary Lou, would you do me a favour?' Katrina was sitting at her desk, phone in her hand, a piece of mango pie by her side. Mary Lou was her best friend. She was married to a real-estate magnate who owned a significant portion of Manhattan.

'Can do,' said Mary Lou, who was in the enviable position of being able to do most anything, including the possible removal of mountains. All you needed, she'd explained once, was time and equipment, and both were for sale.

'Have you ever heard of a Max Laurello?' Katrina asked.

'Max Laurello? No. Is he somebody?'

'He's a writer. Adventure, international intrigue, so he says. He's my neighbour here.'

'Is he good-looking?'

'Very.' Leave it to Mary Lou not to beat around the bushes.

'How old?'

'Middle thirties, I guess.'

'Single?'

Katrina laughed. 'He professes to be plagued by multiple females—wives, mistresses, girlfriends—I have no idea.'

'Oh, one of those.' Disappointment wafted along the line. 'Well, I guess I don't need to worry about you.' Meaning Bastian had furnished her with all the experience of men of the philandering variety to last her a lifetime. So true.

'Nothing to worry about,' Katrina agreed.

'Have you seen these women? Are they with him?'

'Oh, no. He came here to escape them, or so he says.'

'Poor man,' Mary Lou said with mock-pity. 'And now that he's all alone he wants you, because he really can't live without women, no matter how much trouble they are. Would you like me to find you a discreet hit man to take care of him?'

'Mary Lou!' Katrina began to laugh. 'It's a good thing I know you.'

Mary Lou let out a deep sigh. 'I know, I know. I'm a pussy cat at heart. So what would you like me to do?'

'I want you to check with the library and see if they have any of his books. Max Laurello. Write it down.'

'Is that all?' Mary Lou sounded disappointed. Obviously she had hoped for a more intriguing assignment to brighten her day.

'Yep, that's all. Oh, and thanks for the books. The kids love them.'

'Next time you ask for a favour, make it count for something.'

'Like what?'

'Gee, I don't know. Yak butter from Tibet, anything.'

Katrina laughed. 'I'll check my cookbooks for a recipe that uses it.'

'I doubt there is one. The stuff stinks.'

Max came to see her two nights later while she was watching an old film from the Fifties. It was wonderful: the hairdos, the clothes, Cary Grant. Now here was a man she could fall in love with! A gentleman, always.

'I'd like to take a look at your bedroom,' Max stated casually, as if he were asking to borrow a cup of sugar.

She stared at him. 'Pardon me?'

He folded his arms and sighed impatiently. 'I'd like a look at your bedroom.' It sounded more like an order than a request. 'If you don't mind,' he added.

What crazy nonsense was this? What sane man would come into a woman's house and ask to see her bedroom? She straightened her spine and glared at him. 'Yes, I do mind! And, for the record, I'm watching a movie and you're interrupting me! Didn't you once make a point about how much you didn't enjoy being interrupted?'

'You're not working, are you?' he asked with an infuriating lift of his eyebrows. He glanced at the TV screen. 'Black and white?'

'It's very old.' She switched off the VCR.

'Don't let me interfere with your entertainment,' he said generously. 'I'll just run up and have a quick look. I won't touch a thing. I want to see your dressing-table.' He waved his hand. 'Nothing personal, just a little research.'

'Visual inspiration. Spare me. What do you expect to find in my bedroom?'

He shrugged. 'Perfume.'

'Oh, I see. Why don't you just ask me?'

'You'll lie,' he said promptly.

He had a point there. She bit her lip. 'Are you sure?'

'All right, what perfume do you use?'

'Poison,' she said, staring straight into his blue eyes. Poison wasn't what he'd want for his precious Isabel, she who brought the hero back to life.

He crossed his arms in front of his chest. 'I was right, you lied. I'm familiar with that one.'

Used by one of his harem, no doubt. 'If you're looking for a name, there are lots. There's Opium, Obsession, Passion, Seduction, Escape...take your pick.'

'So clever you are.' Uninvited, he parked himself next to her on the sofa and leaned his face towards her. 'And what do you use?' He took in a deep breath through his nose. 'Mmm, nice. What is it?'

'Soap.' He was too close for comfort. She was uncomfortably aware of having nothing on under her kimono; she'd showered and washed her hair and was ready for bed once the film was over.

'I see,' he said, leaning closer yet. He took her hand, turned it over and ran his lips seductively over the inside of her wrist. 'And what, sweet Katrina, do you put on when you go out?'

Her heart was racing at the feel of the sensuous touch of his lips on her skin. She should pull her hand out of his grasp. She should push him away. She should most definitely push him away, preferably all the way off the island into the sea. Strange how helpless she felt, as if some other power had taken over, as if she was in a trance and couldn't move, couldn't do anything. She was under the spell of those blue eyes, that soft, sexy voice. All she was aware of was his presence, the strong male presence, his lips trailing seductively along the inside of her arm.

'Joy by Patou,' she said, relenting, anticipating his response.

He dropped her hand unceremoniously back into her lap and his face lit up as he smiled. 'Perfect!' he said, right on cue. Then he leaned forward again, took her face between his hands and kissed her full on the mouth. 'Thank you. You've got gorgeous lips, by the way. Very kissable.'

He had to hear her heart. It was slamming against her ribs. She stared into his eyes, transfixed, and for the longest time they sat there, looking at each other, wordlessly, breathlessly. Then slowly he lowered his mouth to hers again and kissed her once more, putting his arms around her. This time it was different. It was a deliberately sensual kiss, a kiss that left nothing to the imagination. It overwhelmed her so completely that she sat mesmerised in his embrace.

He released her abruptly. Without a word, he came to his feet, crossed the sitting-room and went out on the veranda. Stunned, she watched him go, then anger rushed in.

What the hell did he think he was doing? Did he think he could barge into her house, demand information, kiss her senseless—just like that?

Apparently he did, and he certainly had.

She took a deep breath. She was shaking all over. It was pitiful! Furiously, she jumped to her feet, went to the kitchen and poured herself a rum punch from the pitcher in the refrigerator, then went back to Cary Grant, the gentleman, always.

Only she couldn't keep her mind on Cary Grant. Her mind was too busy with Max Laurello, whose mouth she could still feel on her lips.

'How much for this place?' Max asked. He'd come up the stairs to the veranda where she was sitting, studying a book about bush medicine and the Caribbean folklore of healing. Very intriguing. He towered over her, looking impatient. She held his eyes and very demonstratively put her book down.

'Oh,' he said, frowning, as if he suddenly remembered his manners. 'Am I disturbing you?'

'Heck, no,' she said lightly. 'I'm just lazing around, not writing a novel or anything serious like that.'

'Well, that's a relief.' He glanced down at the book on the table and read the cover. 'Good lord, what are you doing?'

'Searching for a repellent.'

'A repellent for what?'

'You.'

He cocked a quizzical brow. 'A repellent for me?'

'Right. For someone who doesn't like to be disturbed, you sure have no qualms about disturbing other people. You keep barging in here as if you own the place.' Kissing me as if you have every right to. Her body grew warm at the memory.

'Well, I want to own the place,' he said. 'That's why I'm here. How much do you want for it?'

She stared at him. 'Sorry to disappoint you, but it's not for sale. I live here, remember?'

He leaned casually against one of the veranda posts, legs crossed at the ankles. He wore faded jeans and a black T-shirt that stretched across his broad shoulders. 'I thought you might want to sell it when you went back to the States. I thought you needed money.'

She laughed. 'What I need, in the long run, is a way to make a living, a career, to make myself independent. Starvation is not yet imminent.'

'Money can make you independent. I'll pay you a quarter of a million for this place. American dollars, that is.'

It was a generous offer, certainly. Katrina frowned. 'Why do you want to buy this place? You *have* a house.'

'That's not mine. I'm merely renting it and the lease is up. I've got to be out of it by the end of next week. The owners are coming back.' He crossed his arms in front of his chest. 'I've decided I want my own place on the island so I can come here whenever I want to. And don't tell me to go look for other places because I already did. There isn't exactly a plethora of villas around here, and none of them is available, for rent or sale.'

'And that includes my house,' she said promptly. 'It's not for sale. I guess you're out of luck. You'll have to go back to your harem and finish your book in Vermont.' She could not help feeling a tiny speck of malice.

He glowered at her and she laughed.

'All right,' he said, 'let me rent it from you.'

'I live here. Where am I supposed to go?'

'Back to New York. Didn't you say that's where you are from?'

So she had. But Bastian's New York penthouse apartment had been sold to pay off his gambling debts, as had the chalet in Switzerland and the beach house on the French Riviera, and the ranch in Texas, not to mention his racing cars, his twin-engine plane, his horses, his collection of antique hunting rifles and his pet cheetah. The house of her childhood would be on the market soon.

'I have nowhere to go,' she said. It sounded rather tragic, but it was true.

'All right, stay,' he said generously. 'Just don't——'

'I know, disturb you. Frankly, I can't imagine a worse fate than to stay in the same house with you.' She wouldn't have a moment's peace. Her heart would be working overtime all the time. The idea of him living under the same roof was terrifying.

'You couldn't have a better lodger,' he assured her. 'I'll work all day and won't bother you at all. You won't even know I'm there. I'll tell you what. You give me a couple of rooms, one to work in and one to sleep in. You take care of my meals, you answer the phone and take messages and I'll pay you five hundred per week. American dollars.'

Five hundred a week was two thousand a month. She could use it.

'No,' she said. It was too dangerous. She needed to keep him at a distance. A man like Max would wreak havoc with her emotions.

'Please,' he said.

'No,' she said, steeling herself against the hypnotic blue of his eyes.

The next evening he brought her rainforest orchids, a bottle of French wine and a huge box of Belgian chocolates. He smiled charmingly. His blue eyes were irresistible. All her good sense flew straight out of the window.

'All right, then,' she said.

After all, what was life without a little adventure, a little risk?

He suggested they talk over the details immediately. She was right in the middle of cooking dinner so she asked him to come to the kitchen with her. Needless to say, he had timed his visit perfectly.

'Would you like to stay for dinner?' she asked. It was the polite thing to do. Flowers, wine, chocolate; quite a cache, really.

He gave her a solemn look. 'I don't want to disturb you.'

'Don't push your luck,' she said.

'Yes, thank you, I'd like to stay for dinner,' he said promptly.

She poured him a glass of wine from the bottle she'd opened for herself earlier. She liked sipping a glass of wine while she cooked. The dish for today was wild duck with fresh pineapple and brandy, another of her own creations. He watched her as she busied herself at the stove, and she felt a strange uneasiness, an awareness of herself and him that was quite disturbing. It tickled through her bloodstream like an unpleasant allergy. Well, maybe it was not altogether unpleasant. It added a certain excitement to the atmosphere, a sense of adventure.

'Where did you get the wine and the chocolates?' she asked. Even in Port Royal the stores carried nothing more than the basics, and certainly not expensive bottles of French wine and boxes of imported chocolates.

'From the Plantation. I'm cosy with the manager.'

'Why don't you go stay at the Plantation instead of coming here?'

'The Plantation is booked solid two years in advance.'

Right. It had slipped her mind. She opened the bottle of wine he had given her to give it time to breathe. It was a lovely Côte Rôtie, which would go supremely well with the duck.

He straddled a chair and glanced at the notebook on the table. 'What is this?'

'I'm making notes about this dish. I'm writing a cookbook.'

I'm writing a cookbook. It sounded wonderful! So determined, so purposeful, so creative!

'An excellent idea,' he remarked. 'You'll need someone to test-taste, I presume?'

She stirred the pineapple and brandy sauce. 'And you're offering your services?'

'Since I'm going to be living here, I'm willing to serve as your guinea pig.'

'I'll be much obliged,' she said drily.

'What will you call your book?'

'I'm not sure. I need an angle, though, something that makes it different from all the other cookbooks out there. Something like Gourmet Cooking for the Dispossessed, or Rich Cuisine for the Poor and Lean. You get the idea.'

'I get the idea. However, you may well end up with a marketing problem there—a bit of a discrepancy between product and clientele.'

He had a point. He studied her notes. 'Where do you get these ingredients?'

'From the Plantation. I'm cosy with the chef.'

'And they fly everything in fresh from the States and Europe,' he stated.

'Right. Royalty demands *haute cuisine*.'

The food was ready and they moved to the dining-room. Max poured the wine. She watched his hand around the bottle, a sexy brown hand, strong and competent.

'I have a toast,' he said, raising his glass.

She lifted her glass up to his and their eyes met. For an infinitesimal moment there was silence. 'To a successful, productive and stimulating cohabitation,' he said softly, and suddenly the air seemed electric. His eyes gleamed darkly into hers and, annoyingly, her heart lurched in her chest. She felt an odd premonition—danger, excitement.

Crystal clinked against crystal, a festive, joyous sound, mocking her apprehensions.

'Let's hope it works out,' she said lightly, breaking her gaze away from his eyes and taking a drink from her wine.

The moment passed and they began to eat. The food was done to perfection. Truly masterful, even if she did think so herself. Tomorrow she could type out the final version of her recipe and put it in her book file.

'When will you have the photographs back?' she asked, remembering at the same time that Mary Lou had not yet called her back to inform her of the presence or absence of books written by Max Laurello in the New York City library system.

'Not until a few days from now. I'm having them developed and printed in a lab on Barbados.'

He had done a lot of travelling, it turned out, starting out his career as a photo-journalist. He'd spent time with Berber Nomads in the Sahara, the Masai in Tanzania, and a primitive tribe in Papua New Guinea. He had seen scenes she never had. While she'd languished in five-star hotels on various continents, unhappy, and lonely, he had tramped through the jungles, kayaked down rivers, safaried through the savannahs. He had eaten with tribal chiefs, danced with Amazon Indians, ridden camels through the desert.

It was an adventure just listening to him, watching his face, his eyes, his hands. She laughed, feeling light and free and not a little delirious. He was an amusing man. And so handsome. And his hands, they were so strong.

Somehow, the bottle of wine was empty. It was a delicious wine and she had savoured all of the many sips she had taken. Wine went so easily when there was someone else at the table, someone to talk to, especially an interesting man with stories to tell.

She sighed with contentment. It was so nice to have someone to talk to, someone to laugh with. It was, after all, a pretty lonely business eating by yourself so often. Not that she did it every day; she did have friends on the island and she was invited over, or she invited them.

Yet it would be nice to have a man all of her own, one to eat with every day, one with whom she could share her thoughts, her feelings and a big, happy bed.

A man like Max, came the unbidden thought.

'Is something wrong?' asked Max.

She swallowed hard and managed to produce a bright smile. 'No, nothing at all. Are you ready for dessert?'

He said he was, and she went into the kitchen to collect her next culinary creation, the frozen strawberry mousse she had made the day before. The Plantation head chef, who was French, of course, had offered her the strawberries without her having asked for them. They were about an hour past their peak and he was expecting a fresh supply to be flown in at any moment. Katrina had rushed home and created her mousse, lest the tender fruits would lose any more of their flavour and fervour.

Max examined the mousse, decorated with a sprig of mint. 'And all of this you do for yourself?' he asked, frowning.

'For the moment I'm considering it my profession,' she said grandly. The idea of her lazing on the beach and doing nothing was not a palatable image.

'You should be married so someone can appreciate all this on a daily basis.'

'That would be nice.' But she'd tried marriage once and it hadn't worked like that. She smiled. 'You're moving in next week and you can enjoy my cooking.'

'And I certainly will. Tell me, why are you living alone?' he asked, as if it were merely a matter of choice, rather than a cosmic conspiracy to keep her lonely and unloved.

'I prefer to,' she said, as if she were keeping out an army of handsome, willing men pounding on her door wanting to gain entrance and love her madly.

'Surely there is a man in your life.'

'No,' said Katrina. 'There's no man in my life.' She *was* leading a lonely life. She'd led a lonely life for a long time, but complaining didn't help, did it? A man was not a commodity you purchased in the super-market. Love was not something that you plucked off the trees. She felt tears come to her eyes. She shouldn't have had so much wine. Too much wine made her weepy.

She pushed her chair away. 'I'll get the coffee,' she said huskily, and fled from the room.

The coffee brewed, they sat on the rattan sofa outside on the veranda. The high-pitched shrieking of the crickets and the tree frogs filled the warm evening air. A full moon peeked through the palm trees. The smooth Caribbean sea glimmered in the moonlight. It was all very lovely, very romantic. Her heart was going too fast.

'You ran away from someone, didn't you?' he asked.

'No,' she said. 'I didn't run away from any man. And no man ran away from me, either.' She tried to sound businesslike, but her voice trembled, quite spoiling the effect.

'What did he do to you?'

'Who?'

'Whoever is making you so unhappy. Did he beat you?'

'No. He never laid a finger on me.' He'd hardly touched her at all, at least not after the honeymoon, but she didn't say that.

'Did he drink?'

'Not in excess.' Well, not usually.

'Drugs?'

'No.' It almost made her laugh. Bastian had liked his body too much. He'd worked out all the time. 'There's nobody. I've not been kicked around or kicked out and I'm not a victim of any sort.'

'So why are you crying?' he asked softly.

She swallowed, hating herself for being such a sentimental slob. She wanted laughs in her life, not tears. There'd been enough tears, more than enough. 'I don't know,' she said huskily. 'It must be the mousse. It's not as good as I had expected it to be. All this work for nothing.' She wiped at her eyes, but it was useless. The tears kept right on coming.

'Would you rather not have me move in with you?' he asked. 'Are you sorry you've agreed to it? I know I did rather push you into it. I can find somewhere else to live.'

'No,' she said, blowing her nose. 'I'm a woman of my word. Just ask Bastian.' Oh, God, why had she said that?

'Who's Bastian?'

'Somebody I knew. I made him a promise and kept it for six years.' To love, honour and obey. In as much as he had allowed her to.

'And then you broke it?'

'No. Then he died.'

'I'm sorry,' he said. 'Is that why you are crying?'

'No,' she said, wiping at her eyes again.

'You're confusing me,' he said.

'I'm confusing myself. I shouldn't have had that last glass of wine.'

'Nothing you've said made any sense.'

'You just don't understand,' she said.

He smiled crookedly. 'I never do. They all tell me that.' He wrapped his arms around her and held her tight. It was the most extraordinary feeling. Comfort and warmth. And more, so much more. His body was hard and strong and yet there was tenderness in his embrace and all her senses sprang to life.

'Please don't cry,' he said in her ear. 'I'm very uncomfortable when women cry.' There was a touch of humour in his voice.

'Do they do that a lot?' she whispered. Their closeness was making her light-headed. A sweet yearning unfurled inside her.

'Who?'

It was hard to think. 'All those women you escaped from in Vermont. Do they cry a lot?'

'All the time.'

'Then you should be used to it,' she said. She needed to go on talking, to keep herself from being overwhelmed by the other feelings fighting for attention, feelings she wasn't sure she should be having.

'I suppose I should be.' He sighed, stroking her hair. 'It would be better if I were.'

'Why?'

'It would be cheaper. Every time they cry it ends up costing me money.'

She stiffened in his embrace. 'Well, I don't want your money!'

His arms tightened around her. 'I know,' he said soothingly. 'But you're different.' He moved his mouth closer to her ear. 'Tell me what it is you want.'

She wanted him to kiss her. She wanted to be loved. She wanted one faithful husband and two adorable children. All perfectly normal, healthy, socially responsible desires for a woman of twenty-five.

She couldn't tell him this, of course. Even in the weepy, befuddled state she was in she had enough sense to know that, so instead of talking she cried some more. She couldn't help herself. He handed her his handkerchief.

'What can I do?' he asked. His cheek was touching hers. She felt warmth suffuse her, stirring her blood, a sweet tension taking hold of her body.

'Hold me,' she said. Please, please, don't let me go now, she pleaded silently.

'I am. Does it help?'

'Yes.' She couldn't remember the last time she'd been held. It felt so good. He smelled so nice—a nice manly smell of warm skin and soap. She was aware of a treacherous need taking over, creeping through her—an aching need for more.

'Are you feeling better?' he asked.

'Yes,' she whispered. She stirred against his shoulder, then her mouth touched the warm skin of his neck. A small shudder went through her. Longing swept over her. She closed her eyes again, not fighting it. It felt so good, so dangerous.

He was stroking her hair, her back. She lifted her face to him. 'Max?' she whispered.

'Yes?' His voice was husky, his eyes very dark.

'Please kiss me.'

CHAPTER FOUR

MAX kissed her, his mouth coming down on hers without hesitation—a sensuous and searching kiss that sent a flood of warmth rushing through her body. Ah, such sweet ecstasy! Katrina leaned in to him, returning the kiss without restraint, letting her senses take over, immersing herself in the rapture of the moment. She didn't want to think. She just wanted to feel, to experience, to savour.

She'd never, never felt anything like this before. But then, she'd never, never known a man like Max...

He drew her closer to him, and she fitted so perfectly against him... the heat of his body intoxicating her, the strength of his arms so comforting... A soft, low moan escaped her and his kiss intensified, his tongue playing an erotic little game that left her weak with longing. She felt his hands stroking her back, sensing in his body a hunger matching her own.

They drew apart, breathless, and she leaned against him, feeling like a rag doll without backbone or strength. She smiled against his chest. It was quite a wonderful feeling. He had quite a wonderful chest—strong, comforting, sexy.

Then he was lifting her up in his arms and carrying her into the house and she sighed and closed her eyes, her arms wound around his neck.

'Where's your bedroom?' he asked close by her ear.

Her bedroom. He was carrying her to her bedroom. Warning bells should be ringing, red lights flashing, sirens screaming. They didn't. She knew why: she wasn't scared. Her heart leaped, but it wasn't from fear. How could she be afraid in Max's arms?

'Your bedroom,' he said again. 'Where is it?'

'Down the hall. Second door on the right. I mean left.' She couldn't even think. She didn't want to think. She'd done too much thinking lately. All she wanted to do now was feel. It felt so good just to feel, to allow herself to give in to savouring her senses—the feel of Max's body against hers, the warm smell of his skin, the beating of his heart under her ear pressed against his chest.

He kicked the door open with his foot and the next moment he unceremoniously dropped her on the bed. She felt abandoned for a moment, looking up at him as he loomed over her. She reached out for his hand.

'Stay with me,' she whispered.

His mouth quirked. 'Don't tempt me.'

'Why not?'

'Because, dear Katrina, in the morning you'd hate me for it.' He bent down and swiftly kissed her on the mouth. 'Goodnight, Katrina.'

The next afternoon he arrived with a large bouquet of red roses.

'I wanted to thank you for a lovely dinner,' he said.

'What dinner?' she asked.

'Last night.'

'I don't remember last night,' she said. 'And I would appreciate it if you didn't either.'

He gave her a crooked smile. 'Was my—er—comfort not adequate?'

'Please, don't embarrass me.'

His smile deepened. 'Why does that embarrass you?'

'I'm not in the habit of *asking* for it! Now please——'

In a flash of movement he'd dropped the flowers on the table and wrapped her into his arms and put his mouth expertly on hers. That accomplished, he kissed her. It was not a sedate kiss from a sedate man. It was a sensuous, passionate kiss from a virile, dynamic man and left absolutely nothing to the imagination. His mouth was warm and insistent, his tongue tantalisingly seductive and her heart went wild. Then he let her go.

His blue eyes met hers. 'You didn't ask for this,' he said softly. 'So how was this?'

She couldn't find words. She was, in short, speechless. Her senses were reeling and her blood was singing. Her body was doing all the same things it had been doing last night and she was as sober as a mud brick. Well, she had been up to just a minute ago.

And all that because Max had kissed her. She'd known many sexy, virile men, and they'd left her stone-cold. Why then was Max having this effect on her? It was terrifying! She couldn't let this happen!

He grinned devilishly, turned on his heel and walked off. She stood there, immobilised, feeling like a fool. Well, she was. The man could kiss, and she hadn't been kissed much lately. Not at all, to be accurate. No wonder her senses were having a party! She had deprived them miserably.

She sagged into a chair and composed her thoughts, which was not easily accomplished. She had to give him credit; he hadn't taken advantage of her fragile emotional state last night, and it would have been easy. Not every man would have felt so obliged. But then, Max was no ordinary man, was he?

And her feelings for him were not so ordinary, either.

One more week and he was moving in with her. What had she done? What *had* she done? It was never going to work. It was madness! What had possessed her to bring into her quiet island home, her haven of tranquillity, an obsessed writer of adventure novels, an expert kisser, a womaniser?

She picked up her Caribbean book of magic brews and healing potions and found the index. What she needed was something strong and powerful to save her from herself.

'We can go into business together,' said Sasha over tea the next day. They were at the Plantation, sitting at a small table in the cobbled courtyard having a proper British afternoon tea. 'Your line of fresh herbs could fit in very well with my cheese. The same market, for one, and I've got that figured out now. We can advertise and ship together.'

Katrina's heart skipped a beat. She'd not expected this offer. She'd come to Sasha for advice. Sasha, after all, was a businesswoman with experience. She'd owned her own clothing boutiques in Connecticut and New York City; in Ghana, West Africa, where she'd gone to visit her niece, she'd started a small clothing export business and found herself a husband at the same time. Now she was into goat's cheese, and successfully so. A woman of many talents, indeed.

What could be better than going into business with Sasha Grant? It was difficult to keep her excitement under control.

'Would you really?' Katrina asked.

Sasha put her fork down. 'I'd like to look into it, but I think it could work very well. We need to make a business plan, of course, get some financial projections. And think of it, you'll be doing something good for the island.'

'How's that?'

'Diversifying the economy, creating jobs.'

She hadn't thought of it that way, but the idea was quite exhilarating. Imagine her, Katrina MacKenzie, diversifying the economy of an entire country! Granted, it was only a tiny island, but still!

Sasha drank the last of her tea and pushed the delicate cup and saucer aside. 'The place is so beautiful, it's hard to remember sometimes how really poor it is,' she said.

Katrina had to admit this was true. She'd have work for several people. People with families, children.

They ordered another pot of tea and more rum cakes with cream and they talked and talked. There was an awful lot to do.

Several days later Katrina still had not heard from Mary Lou. She picked up the phone and dialled New York. Madam was not in, she was told by a maid with a southern accent. There'd been a wonderful snow fall in St Moritz, Switzerland, and madam had departed to go skiing.

Max moved in on Saturday morning. Katrina made herself scarce and went sailing with friends for the day. When she came home late that afternoon, she found him all settled. The computer was set up and the photos were tagged to the bulletin boards, including the ones he'd taken at the orphanage. As promised he'd given her a set of copies and she could only admit that they were wonderful—very professional images evoking a variety of emotions—laughter, sadness, joy. She loved the pictures of herself with the children on her lap and by her side.

Max was banging on the keyboard, typing away, not noticing her standing in the doorway.

'I'm home,' she said from the open doorway.

His head jerked around to look at her. His eyes appeared a little glassy, as if he was not focusing on her, which was probably quite an accurate assessment.

'Great,' he said absently, glancing back at the screen. 'Are you hungry?'

'No. I mean yes, actually.'

'I'll fix us something to eat.'

He made an unintelligible grunt and she turned, annoyed. He'd barely looked at her, barely noticed her at all. He was totally absorbed in his writing. It was as if he were residing somewhere else, as if his mind had completely left the here and now. Well, of course it had. It was residing in the fictitious world of his book, and she, after all, was not in it. Isabel was.

She got some lettuce from the garden, washed it and arranged a big bed of it on two large plates. She'd made some *ceviche* the night before, shrimp and white fish marinated in a mixture of lime juice, sliced onion, garlic, and other seasonings. She divided it between the two plates and sprinkled it with chopped parsley. She sliced a ripe avocado and arranged the wedges around the seafood salad and dinner was ready.

Quickly, she set the table, took a chilled bottle of white wine out of the refrigerator, and sliced some crusty bread.

Max ate with obvious appetite, but he spoke little, his mind busy working, adventuring in the jungles of the Amazon or the deserts of Africa. She couldn't help feeling a little let down. Sitting across the table from a silent man with his mind on other things was about as stimulating as eating by yourself.

It was not a stimulating weekend, but then, he'd moved in to work, not to stimulate her.

On Monday the phone calls began. Max had asked her to answer the phone and take messages if the calls were for him. No problem, she'd said, poor naïve thing that she was.

What she had not expected was to be inundated with calls. From women, all of them. There was a Rebecca,

a Tammy, a Joanna, and a Kelly. They all wanted Max.
To speak to Max. To speak to Max *immediately*. It was
of the *utmost* importance. They spoke to her in turn in
various moods and voices—angry, arrogant, haughty,
pleading, belligerent, as if she, Katrina, were a mere
servant, an unaccommodating servant unwilling to do
their bidding and drag Max out of his study to the phone.

In the days that followed, she took the calls dutifully,
politely, like the perfect secretary she wasn't. After all,
she'd agreed to his deal. She wrote the messages on a
pad in a very businesslike manner. After all, none of this
had anything to do with her.

PLEASE CALL KELLY IN SAN FRANCISCO.
URGENT!

PLEASE CALL TAMMY IN VERMONT.
URGENT!

PLEASE CALL REBECCA IN NEW YORK.
URGENT!

PLEASE CALL JOANNA AT HOME. URGENT!

'I don't want to leave a message,' a husky-voiced
Rebecca stated one morning. 'Where is he?'

'In the study, working.'

'In what study? Where is he staying? Is this a hotel?'

'No,' said Katrina, 'this is a private villa.'

'And who are you?'

'I am the owner of the villa.'

Silence. Katrina coughed politely.

'You mean Max is living with you?' Rebecca enquired.

Katrina considered this. In a manner of speaking, of
course, Max was living with her. 'Yes,' she said. She
could not help a little mischief of her own. After all, she
wasn't lying, was she? And what was one more woman?

The voices were all young and cultured, although not
always polite. One was rather husky, which sounded quite

sexy. Another was light and breathless, a third had a sing-song tone to it. The fourth sounded chic but snobby.

She imagined faces and bodies to go with the voices. They all had long hair, shiny and silky—chestnut, blonde, sable-brown, coppery red. Their eyes were violet-blue, warm hazel, crystalline green, silvery grey. They had long, shapely legs and luscious, curvaceous bodies. It was downright demoralising.

Then a comforting thought occurred to her—a delightful thought, a gift from the stars: none of these gorgeous creatures was—for the moment—living with Max. She, Katrina, was.

Well, so what? She didn't even want him.

He was holed up in the study and worked all day, sometimes half the night. It was very impressive. She could only imagine how impressive his headaches had to be from staring at the computer monitor screen all day. Now and then he'd come out and make himself a cup of coffee, or return one of the phone calls he had received. More often he'd search Katrina out to ask her a question.

What kind of hobbies did she have besides cooking and reading and making up revolting herbal potions? What did she think about the economic situation, about women in the army, about wearing fur coats? What kind of nightgown did she wear? Cotton? Silk? Or did she wear pyjamas or perhaps sleep in the nude?

'Don't you think you're getting a little personal for a mere lodger?' she asked.

He frowned, looking absent-minded. 'Sorry, it was merely an academic question.'

'Research?'

He nodded. 'Yes.'

'I am not interested in being the object of your research,' she said coolly.

'It's not about *you*,' he said, 'it's about Isabel.'

She was getting truly sick of Isabel. 'From all those phone calls I take for you, I gather you have enough experience about women's nightwear that you don't need me to answer questions like that.'

'Isabel is different.'

She groaned. 'Oh, please, spare me.'

'What do you wear in bed?'

'It's none of your business.'

'Then you'll leave me no choice but to sneak into your bedroom one night and have a look for myself.'

'I wear a T-shirt with a slogan.'

He frowned. He was not pleased. 'And what does it say?'

'"Over my dead body" in five languages.'

By the end of the first week she was quite fed up with him as well as with his stable of women. Every time at dinner she would place the messages next to his plate if he had neglected to pick them up by the phone. He would look at them and grunt or frown, then make some calls, or not, depending on his mood.

The next day it would start all over again. It was not always easy to stay polite when one more breathless female voice demanded to speak to Max.

'I'm sorry, he cannot be disturbed, but I'll give him a message if you like.' She was beginning to sound like a broken record.

'That's what you keep telling me! Who the hell are you, anyway?' the woman snarled.

'I'm Max's inspirational assistant,' she said evenly, biting her lip, trying not to laugh.

'You're *what*?'

'His inspirational assistant.'

'I'll bet! Well, tell him I called and that I need to speak to him *immediately* about some very *uninspirational* news. Tell him a tree fell on the roof and it's leaking!'

Get it fixed, Katrina said silently, but, polite person that she was, she didn't say the words out loud. What did this fool of a woman think Max was going to do about a leaky roof in Vermont? 'I will give him the message,' she said politely. 'In the meantime, I suggest you call a roofer.'

What had happened to her peace and solitude? What had happened to the grand notion that she would sort out her emotions, her life, her destiny? There was no quiet. The house was filled with sound—unfamiliar music, an impatient male voice, the phone ringing and ringing and ringing...

She went back to the kitchen, where she was preparing dinner. She must be out of her mind to go through all this trouble feeding him. Well, she wasn't doing it for him, she was doing it for herself. She loved cooking, after all, and there was an endless number of recipes to test for her book.

The next morning one of the women called from Paris. Katrina took down the message and the phone number. It was still there when it was dinnertime and she placed it next to Max's plate.

He came out and sat down, glancing at the note.

'Paris!' he shouted. 'What in the world is she doing in Paris?'

'I didn't consider it my place to ask,' Katrina said and sipped her wine. 'Perhaps she was whisked away by a romantic French count who's sensitive and understanding. You not being there for her and all,' she added helpfully.

He gave her a baleful look. 'No way.'

'You're pretty sure of yourself, aren't you?' she asked.

'If she ran away with anybody, it's more likely to be with a mad drummer.' He cursed under his breath and jumped up from his chair, note in hand.

'You can't call now,' Katrina said reasonably. 'It's the middle of the night in Paris. They'll be in bed.' She couldn't help herself.

'Do you think this is funny?' he asked, giving her a threatening look.

She looked at him wide-eyed. 'I don't know. Is it?'

He didn't answer.

'It must be quite a job keeping track of all these women,' she said, pseudo-sympathetic. 'Not to speak of keeping them all happy.'

'I do my best.' He smiled and took a bite from his food.

'Well, let me tell you what I think,' she began. She felt the swelling of a tide inside her, the accumulation of irritation and anger. 'I don't think it is funny, no. I think it's all quite reprehensible. You're depraved.' She took a fortifying gulp of wine and let him have it. It was not difficult. Having been married to Bastian, she'd had many opportunities for similar speeches.

Her heart was racing, her hands trembled. She was full of righteous indignation and held forth, quite eloquently, about men sleeping around, men with tiny minds and shaky egos. About moral responsibility and lack of values. About the moral decline of modern society. It was quite a tirade and the more she went on, the easier the words came. Words like mindless copulation, carnal pleasures, the exploitation of the female. On and on she went.

It was very satisfying and, having got it off her chest, she felt considerably better. Leaning back in her chair, she gave Max a challenging look.

'Well, well, that was quite a sermon,' he said evenly. He had listened with admirable composure. 'I hadn't realised you were such a high-minded person and such an expert on the subject of debauchery.'

'Oh, I'm an expert all right.' She took the wine bottle and filled her glass. 'One of the best.' She took a drink.

He narrowed his eyes. 'What is that supposed to mean?'

'Exactly what it is meant to mean.' She pushed her chair away from the table. 'Somehow I lost my appetite.'

'Too bad,' he said. 'It does look delicious.'

It had better be. It had cost her three hours to prepare. She walked out of the room and up the stairs. In her room she threw herself on the bed and wept.

Max wasn't any better than Bastian.

The next morning, Tammy called demanding to speak to Max.

'I'm sorry but he's working and can't be disturbed,' Katrina said automatically. 'I'll give him...'

Tammy wanted to hear none of it. 'I want to talk to him now! Now! Now!' she screamed over the phone. Katrina held the receiver away from her ear.

'I'll give him a message,' she said dutifully when the shouting had stopped.

Silence. 'All right, you do that.' The voice had taken on a dangerous calmness. 'Just tell him I'm pregnant and want to know what he thinks we should do about it.' The line went dead.

Katrina felt her heart sink. Tammy was pregnant. Whoever Tammy was. His wife, his mistress, one of his girlfriends. She had the feeling, just hearing the tone of Tammy's voice as she had imparted this juicy bit of information, that Max was not expected to be delighted with the news.

Katrina felt sick, which was strange. After all, she wasn't the one pregnant. She took the pad and began to write. 'Tammy called. She says she is pregnant and needs to speak to you immediately.' Her hand shook. It annoyed her. What did she care about this?

She stared at the note. This might be one of the kind you didn't leave around waiting to give at lunch or dinner. Her legs felt like wood as she moved to Max's office. She knocked and entered at his impatient growl.

'I have an important message for you,' she said to his back. She heard the hollow tone in her voice, echoing the hollow feeling in her chest.

'I told you not to disturb me, dammit!' His hands kept flying over the keyboard, his eyes intent on the screen.

She did not like being cursed at. As a matter of fact, it made her quite cranky. Her blood began to pump and she momentarily lost all capacity to think. A demon took over her mind and did it for her. She walked up to Max and slammed her hand down on his. The computer squealed in warning.

For one terrifying moment there was utter silence. A silence so loaded, only a spontaneous combustion of some sort would relieve the pressure. Needless to say, Max would do the honours.

In a flash of movement he was out of his chair, standing over her, his face a frightening mask of fury. 'What the hell do you think you're doing?' he asked, his voice rough with rage.

'I made you stop working,' she said reasonably. She didn't feel very reasonable. As a matter of fact, she felt terrified. Her insides felt liquid with fear. Her legs trembled, her heart raced, her head throbbed. She was a mess.

'Don't you ever, *ever* do that again!' His voice now was low and dark with threat.

She fought to keep in control. She stared straight back into his face. 'And don't you ever, *ever* curse at me again,' she returned, willing her voice to stay steady. It was, almost.

'I told you specifically that I do not want to be disturbed!'

She took a deep breath and straightened her spine. 'And I decided to do it anyway.' Miracles of miracles, she had managed to hold on to the note and it was still in her hand. She thrust it at him. 'I decided that this was a message that should not lie around all day. I think you'd better read it.'

He took the paper and scanned the words. Under his tan, his face lost all colour. In two flying leaps he was out of the room. Moments later she heard his voice reverberating through the house. 'All we need is a baby in the house!' he shouted. 'Are you out of your mind?' Obviously, impending fatherhood did not delight him. It wouldn't have delighted Bastian, either. She felt a flare of pain and fury, mixed. She took a deep breath and closed her eyes.

'How did this happen?' she heard him ask furiously. 'After all the talks we had, how could you do this? I thought you understood! For God's sake, where are your brains?'

Katrina clenched her hands by her side. She hated him. She knew she did. She hated all men from now until eternity. They were selfish and arrogant and despicable.

There was a short silence.

'It's a good thing you're not in the same room with me, Tammy, girl, because I'd wring your neck!' He listened for a moment. 'No, I am *not* prepared to discuss this now! I am trying to write a book! If you keep calling me I'll never get it finished! I'll talk to you when I am good and ready!' Katrina heard the receiver hit its cradle in quite an ungentle fashion. A moment later Max came storming back into his office, where she was still standing, rooted to the spot.

She unglued her feet from the floor. 'I'm not taking any more phone calls for you,' she said, and walked out. She was too furious to speak any further.

She spent the rest of the day at the beach, conveniently leaving the cordless phone at the house. Let him answer his own calls or invest in his own answering machine. She took a long swim and eventually she managed to calm herself down enough to read.

The peace and quiet were bliss, the chocolates were delicious, and her book afforded her a wonderful escape: somewhere alone in Alaska, with a dedicated doctor to the Eskimos, a man with a conscience, an even temperament and no harem.

Tropical dusks were short and swift, and she packed up her things about six and went back to the house. All was silent. No music, no telephone. She tiptoed by the door to Max's study and heard the rhythmic clicking of the keyboard. He was still at it. Good. She could just imagine the kind of adventure book he was writing. Full of sex and violence and disgusting human beings without a scrap of moral values.

She had a shower, washed her hair, lotioned her skin all over and put on a long loose caftan. She ate a banana, looking defiantly at the refrigerator. She wasn't hungry. She didn't feel like cooking. So she wasn't going to. Let him go hungry.

She went into the living-room and selected a film to watch on the VCR. Halfway through she paused it and went to the kitchen to make a cup of coffee. Still no sign of Max. Good.

She had only just settled herself again when she heard his footsteps come down the corridor. On the screen, the hero kissed the heroine. The heroine, eyes flashing, slapped the hero in the face. Max came into the room.

'You women,' said Max cheerily, 'always yelling, always slapping. It's not easy being a man.'

Anger flared up again, burning her throat. 'Get lost,' she said succinctly.

'What about my dinner?'

'Cook your own dinner.' She glared at him defiantly.

His eyebrows rose imperiously. 'Correct me if I'm wrong, but I believe we have an agreement.'

She switched the VCR off. 'I'm not answering the phone and I'm not cooking your dinner. I am not one of your women. I am not your servant. If you don't like it here, by all means go somewhere else.'

He feigned a look of surprise. 'What's the matter with you?'

'What's the matter with *me*? I should be asking *you* that question! I suppose you already forgot that phone call you made this morning? What kind of way is that to talk to a pregnant woman? And don't tell me I shouldn't be listening to other people's conversations, because there was no avoiding it! They could hear you in Rome! You're an obnoxious, selfish bastard!' So there. It felt good to have said it.

He frowned. 'Oh, yes, I remember now. Tammy. It was Tammy, wasn't it?'

'Yes, Tammy! Your wife back home, or one of your girlfriends or whoever she is. You had the gall to tell her you were not prepared to discuss it. You were writing a book. Pestilence or pregnancy, *nothing* should stand in the way of your precious book! Pregnant Tammy will just have to wait!'

He sat down in a chair, stretched out his legs and smiled. 'Tammy is a piece of work.'

'A pregnant piece of work, and the way you talked to her was abominable! I don't understand what these women *see* in you, why they keep calling you! They act as if they can't live without you!'

'Well, they can't. Not very well, at any rate.' He was smiling. So happy, so satisfied with his work, his life, so full of fun and cheer.

She wanted to hit him.

Then again, who cared? Not she. She'd learned her lesson. If these women were dumb enough to want him, they were welcome to him. That was what she had thought of Bastian and his women. She was sick and tired of womanisers. Men who needed women to validate them. Men whose egos depended on their sexual conquests.

'I'm starving,' he said again. 'Let's find us some dinner at the Plantation. I feel like a long, leisurely meal with a nice bottle of wine.'

'I don't suppose you'd want to toast to your up-coming fatherhood?' she said sarcastically.

'No, I wouldn't,' he said easily. 'Tonight I'd just like to relax for a while.'

'While Tammy is weeping her heart out.'

'Tammy isn't weeping,' he said. 'She's angry, but she'll get over it.' He smiled again, a gleam of humour in his eyes.

A most uncomfortable feeling began to seep through her. Something wasn't quite right. There was something in his eyes, his smile.

He was egging her on.

'What's so funny?' she demanded.

'You,' he said. 'You, getting all worked up about somebody you don't even know, knowing no facts, no background, hearing a one-sided conversation and jumping to all the wrong conclusions.'

'When somebody tells me she's pregnant, I don't have to do any jumping in order to know that she's pregnant!'

'You shouldn't believe everything you hear,' he said evenly.

'And what is that supposed to mean?'

'Tammy isn't pregnant. It was merely a ploy to get me to the phone. An exceedingly successful ploy, I must admit. Tammy, by the way, is my sixteen-year-old sister and what she wanted to discuss was the subject of her having her own car, financed by me, of course. And that, dear Katrina, was the subject I was not prepared to discuss.' He smiled again, victorious. 'Shall we go out and have some dinner?'

So there it was: Katrina and her big mouth put in her place. There was no gracious way out, so she dropped the subject like a hot brick.

'Actually, I'm starving,' she said brightly, feeling dizzy with relief. 'Dinner is an excellent idea.'

Forty-five minutes later they were sitting in the lap of luxury at the Plantation restaurant, wine in hand, enjoying the ambience. The restaurant was the large, wrap-around veranda of the old Plantation Great House. The building was hundreds of years old and had originally been the elegant Great House of a large sugar-cane plantation.

A cool evening breeze wafted across the veranda, carrying with it the seductive scents of tropical blooms. Palm fronds rustled gently and the moon silvered the placid Caribbean sea.

Max was in an excellent mood. He was charming, polite, entertaining. He told her she looked gorgeous.

She wore a playful little dress she'd bought in Paris a year ago, a confection of flaming fuchsia silk, with off-

the-shoulder sleeves and a short, swirly skirt. It made
her feel cheerful and light-hearted, a mood not easily
acquired after making a fool of yourself.

Over a first course of artichoke heart stuffed with
lobster, Katrina found out the identity of the other
women who had been haunting the phone. Sisters, every
one of them. Or, more correctly, half-sisters.

Max had no wife, no children, no girlfriend, no mistress. All he had was a big house in Vermont peopled
with a grandmother, a mother and four half-sisters, who
at the moment were roaming around the country for
various and sundry reasons. Katrina's anger turned into
instant pity.

No wonder he had fled to St Barlow!

However, her pity did not last long at the thought of
what he had done to her, naïve Katrina. All week he had
strung her along, leaving her to her delusionary fantasies without giving her a hint towards the truth. He'd
pretended innocence, feigned absent-mindedness and
been purposely obtuse, all to allow her to make a fool
of herself. And she had done it splendidly. She had truly
risen to the occasion, giving him a sermon on morals
worthy of an eighteenth-century hell-and-brimstone
preacher. It was not an incident she wanted to dwell on.
She did not normally wish for holes in the ground into
which she could disappear, but she was coming mighty
close tonight.

'What happened to all the males in the family?' she
asked, diverting her thoughts from humiliation and
mortification. He told her that his own father had left
him and his mother in order to join the French Foreign
Legion in search of an adventurous life. Domesticity,
babies and nappies had not agreed with him. Max had
been three months old. Nine years later his mother had
married a man of a more steady nature, a dairy farmer

called Tom, who couldn't leave even for a weekend because his cows needed milking. They had four daughters: Rebecca, Joanna, Kelly and Tammy. They were very happy until Tom had been killed in a freak accident several years ago.

'So you're the head of the family, so to speak,' Katrina concluded insightfully.

'So they all seem to think,' he said and smiled crookedly.

It was a wonderful dinner. The candle flickered intimately. The heady scent of flowering jasmine wafted around them. A soft breeze stirred the air. The ginger mousse with chocolate sauce was divine.

She felt bewitched, enchanted. His smile warmed her blood. His voice stirred her senses. And why not? After all, he was a man of virtue, a man who took his responsibilities seriously, a man who took care of a grandmother, a mother, and four spoiled-rotten half-sisters. How could she not fall in love with him?

Upon their return to the villa, the beach looked inviting, the soft sand glimmering white in the light of the moon.

'Let's stay out for a while,' he suggested, and she took off her high heels and followed him down the path to the beach. She stepped in the warm water, which lapped softly around her ankles. She had the sudden urge to take her clothes off and float in the water and look up at the stars.

Better not. Seeing her skinny body naked might make Max take off screaming for the mountains. Five more pounds and she'd give it a try. Well, maybe. She smiled at her own reckless thoughts. Tempting a man like Max was playing with fire.

Of course, playing with fire had its charm.

She turned to see Max sitting in the sand, observing her, and she plopped herself down next to him, not caring about her dress. The sand was soft. The dress would survive.

They sat in silence for a while, listening to the soft sounds of the water, watching the sky, feeling tension build between them. They were sitting so close, so dangerously close, yet not touching. Every cell of her body seemed to quiver with anticipation. She tried not to think about him touching her, about his hard body against her own.

Instead, she thought of the past week, about all the phone calls, about the sermon she had preached him.

'I owe you an apology,' she said. 'I've said some pretty awful things to you.'

'But you said them so well,' he said, smiling crookedly.

She laughed and he took her hand. It was warm and strong and his touch sent an electric shiver through her, setting off a flood of warmth.

'Besides,' he went on, 'I asked for it fair and square. I quite enjoyed leading you on. It was a dastardly thing to do, but I hope you can forgive me.' Then he drew her close and kissed her.

The heat of his mouth sent a wave of tingling delight all through her body. He kissed the way he did everything else—purposeful and determined. There was nothing tentative about him and he took charge of her completely, pushing her back so she lay in the sand and leaning over her so there was no way to go. Not that she wanted to. Her body melted into the sand, weightless, caught in a spell of delicious sensations.

What could she do but give in? She was all alone with him on a soft tropical beach on an idyllic island with the moon overhead and not a soul around in miles. Alone with six feet two of masculine power and sex appeal.

And not just any six feet two of masculine power and sex appeal.

Max. Max, who made her feel as no man ever had. Max who did things to her heart and body she'd never experienced before. Max, with whom she was falling hopelessly, helplessly in love.

Why struggle and ruin her expensive dress? Surrender was the only choice, really.

CHAPTER FIVE

IT WAS magic.

Max's mouth, determined, yet tender, played with hers as if it were a delicate instrument. His lips stroked hers with sweet temptation, his tongue tantalised hers in an erotic little dance of pleasure that set off a storm of longing inside her.

'Oh,' she breathed, feeling blissfully delirious. He put his arms around her more fully and turned her on her side, pressing her body against his, still kissing her with a warm, passionate urgency that shook her to the core.

She had never been kissed with such an intoxicating mixture of warmth and caring and passion. On and on, while his hand stroked her hair, her back, while his taut body moved restlessly against her own heated one. Then they both stilled, breathless, silent, clinging to each other.

So many hidden yearnings, so many secret longings . . . She felt overwhelmed with emotion, an odd, indescribable feeling that seemed to well up from the very depth of her being and brought tears to her eyes. And then, without any warning, she was crying—tears running hot down her face. Her body went rigid trying to control it, yet there was nothing she could do against the wave of emotion washing over her.

His face turned slightly, his mouth touching her cheek. For a moment he was perfectly still, not even breathing.

'Katrina?' he asked softly, incredulously. 'Are you crying?'

Words would not come out of her mouth. She nodded.

'Why?'

'I don't know,' she whispered. She didn't. It was the craziest thing that had ever happened to her.

'Was I that bad?'

Despite the tears, she smiled. 'No, no. You were...wonderful.'

'So wonderful I moved you to tears! Well, there's a first time for everything.'

She took a shuddering breath. 'You kissed me as if...'

'As if what?'

'You kissed me as if you meant it.'

He laughed with warm amusement. 'I most certainly did. Why else would I do it?'

Out of duty, came the silent answer. But of course that was nonsense. Max was under no obligation to kiss her. That had been Bastian's territory. He'd kissed her and made love to her out of duty. Because he thought she wanted it, because, after all, they were husband and wife and it wasn't all that great a sacrifice once or twice a year when he happened to be home. She didn't want to think of Bastian, the happy-go-lucky philanderer, Bastian, the hedonist.

Max was still holding her and it was the most wonderful, safe, warm feeling. Then his hand moved to her chin and lifted it towards him. 'You want to try it again?' he whispered.

She nodded silently.

'Are you going to cry again?'

'I don't know. I don't think so.'

His mouth moved over hers again and she let herself be swept away once more, let her own need express itself as she kissed him back, holding him tight.

'Wow,' he said. 'You kissed me as if you meant it.'

'I did.' It was quite frightening, the intensity of her feelings. She sat up and took a deep breath, trying to take control of herself. She should think of something unromantic, but not one unromantic thing came into her head. All she was aware of was the man next to her, the seductive lapping of the sea and the bright glitter of stars. It was a conspiracy. She took another deep breath.

'Why aren't you married?' she asked to break the silence.

He groaned. 'I have a grandmother, a mother and four sisters. One more woman in my life and they can lock me up in a padded room.'

She laughed. 'Maybe you ought to find husbands for all of them and get them off your back.'

'That idea has occurred to me, but who'd want them?'

She pretended not to hear the humour in his voice. 'That bad, is it? Well, you may have to pay them off— the men, that is, of course. It's done all the time. Arranged marriages, I mean.' How did she manage to sound so casual?

He frowned. 'It's a thought.'

'And when you're free of them you can find yourself a wife, an obedient, docile type who won't disturb you while you work. Someone who'll make herself invisible until you snap your fingers. A traditional oriental girl would do the trick, although I'm not sure there are many left. Women's lib is catching on everywhere and——'

He grabbed her suddenly and turned her on her back in the sand, and kissed her with unrestrained passion, making her blood go wild once more. When he was done she felt thoroughly ravished, which no doubt had been his intention.

'Do you think,' he said darkly, 'that I am the kind of man who wants a docile woman?'

'No, I suppose not. You'd scare her to death.'

He laughed. 'Do I scare you?'

'Not for a minute.' It was a lie. She was terrified. Terrified about the emotions he evoked in her, about the sensations he stirred up in her body. A sweet, delicious terror, but terror none the less.

'Good.' His mouth travelled down her throat to the top of her breasts. She closed her eyes. His tongue was warm and moist on her skin, a velvety, erotic touch— the more so because he made no attempt to pull down the bodice of her dress to expose her breasts in their entirety. It would take no effort at all and he knew it.

It was hard to breathe. With her eyes closed, she stroked the back of his head, trailing her fingers through his thick hair. After a while he moved back up to her mouth, making a trail of damp little kisses.

'Yesterday,' he murmured against her lips, 'you suggested that you were quite an expert on the ways of philandering men.' His tongue traced her mouth. 'How did you come by that?'

'I was married to one,' she said without thinking.

'*Married*?' He lifted his head abruptly. 'You told me you had no husband and you weren't divorced.'

'I don't, I'm not. I'm a widow.' It sounded so strange still.

'I see. The one you made the promise to that you kept for six years.'

'Yes.'

'And he cheated on you.'

Among other things. She squirmed beneath him. 'Please, I don't want to talk about it.' It would spoil everything. It would sour the evening, shrivel the moon, ice up the warm Caribbean waters. She'd been passionately kissed by Max, an experience to savour and cherish, and she wanted nothing to mar the perfection of the moment.

'All right, we won't talk about it.' He took her hand and pulled her to her feet. He put his arms around her and held her tight for a moment. Then he took her hand and they walked silently back up to the house.

They went inside, and he went to his office to work and she went to bed to sleep. Well, that was the idea.

It didn't work, of course. She couldn't sleep. His kiss had aroused disturbing passions in her—wild and delicious. She kept feeling his mouth on hers. She wondered what it would feel like to have his hand caress her bare body. What it would be like to make love with him. She sighed longingly and closed her eyes. He was in his office writing. She fantasised about slipping into his study, tiptoeing up to his chair and putting her arms around him and...

No. It would never work. He did not want to be disturbed when he was writing.

He most certainly did not.

She was out of her mind to have these crazy thoughts. She, poor, love-starved Katrina, going berserk over a couple of sexy kisses from a man who was overdosed on women and their demands on his time. How utterly pathetic!

He had no time. Even at this late hour of the night he was in his study working. And he was probably writing about kissing Isabel on the beach, taking off her clothes, stroking her satiny skin and looking into the deep, secret pools of her eyes. Isabel the paragon.

And she, Katrina, had been merely used for inspiration. She moaned into her pillow. It was an unbearable thought.

The next morning she stood on the bathroom scales and watched the needle with elation. She had gained three pounds in the last week. It was wonderful. Old Doc Whepple would be proud of her. Katrina looked in the mirror, examining her body. It still looked too thin, too virginal, too innocent. Not the body of a widow. She,

Katrina MacKenzie, was a widow. It sounded ridiculous. She simply could not get used to it. The word widow evoked images of blue-haired ladies living in Florida condominiums, of small, shrivelled-up grandmas shrouded in black in Spanish villages.

She could not think of herself as a widow, but here she was, twenty-five years old, and her husband was dead, shot by a bullet meant for a bush pig. During the course of her six-year marriage, she had often dreamed of being free again, but, to be honest, and to her credit, widowhood had not featured in her fantasies. Whatever Bastian might have deserved, such a tragic fate she had never wished him.

The truth was that theirs had not been a happy marriage, a marriage not made in heaven, but in an opulent business office by men in well-cut three-piece suits. Men with money, power and influence, one of whom had been, of course, her father trying to pull off a good business deal. The other one had been Bastian's father, trying to find a way to tame his wild son and make a responsible person out of him.

Arranged marriages, Katrina knew, were not merely events that took place in exotic, far-away places. They happened in modern America and hers had been one of them, although at the time it had not occurred to her to consider it that way. After all, Bastian was a much drooled-over bachelor playboy and she'd imagined herself to be passionately in love with him. She hadn't recognised how shallow and weak he was until it was too late.

Katrina and Max were having a goat's cheese and fruit salad lunch when a package was delivered to the house. It was not easy sitting at the same table with Max and making polite conversation. It was difficult to concentrate on island politics or the blizzard in Chicago while she was watching his hands as he cut his food, watching his mouth as he chewed. She kept thinking about him kissing her, about his hands touching her.

She was falling in love.

It was terrible.

It was dangerous.

It was wonderful.

She looked at the package, relieved by the distraction. It was from Mary Lou.

'Great!' she said, knowing what was in it. She took her knife and sliced open the big padded envelope and took out the two video tapes.

'What are they?' asked Max.

'Movies. My friend Mary Lou taped them for me.'

He picked one of the tapes up and read the hand-written label. He glanced up at Katrina, brow quirked in disbelief.

'*Doris Day*? You had a friend tape Doris Day movies for you?'

'What's wrong with Doris Day?'

'Wasn't she before your time?'

'So were Mozart, Rembrandt and Shakespeare.'

He laughed. '*Touché*. So what do you like about these movies?'

She dabbed her mouth with a napkin. 'They're romantic and upbeat and they always have a happy ending. And of course the leading men are always wonderful.' Cary Grant was one of them.

'You like romantic and upbeat?'

'Yes.' She smiled brightly.

'I see.' A far-away, brooding look came into his eyes. She knew that look and she didn't like it. It took care of all her romantic feelings for him, which, on second thoughts, was just as well. He was too difficult a man to fall in love with. He was infuriating and unbearable most of the time. Well, maybe not most of the time. And for honesty's sake, and she was an honest person, she had to admit that he had his moments. He could be a true gentleman, an interesting conversationalist, and when he kissed her...

She stopped herself right there. She did not want to linger on the more passionate side of his nature, not over goat's cheese and fruit.

He put down his fork and leaned back in his chair, deep blue eyes scrutinising her, searching for her soul. 'So you like things romantic and upbeat. What about reality?'

'I'm overdosed on reality. I need fantasy for a break. Fantasising is good for the soul.' She speared a slice of papaya and ate it.

'You do a lot of fantasising?'

'Oh, yes, all the time.' She smiled sweetly, knowing what would come next.

'What do you fantasise about?' he asked right on cue.

'Oh, all sorts of things. What I would do if I were president of the United States, for instance,' she lied. She smiled loftily. 'Does Isabel fantasise a lot?'

There was a gleam of humour in his eyes. 'I'm considering it.'

'She wouldn't fantasise about being president, probably.' She ate a slice of mango. 'She might fantasise about men. Many men, and going on treks through the jungles with them. And they all develop passionate desires for her and she has to...'

'Shut up, Katrina.'

'Oh, thank you. I'm only trying to do my job as your inspirational assistant.' She threw him a baleful look and got up from the table. 'Well, I won't bother you any more.' Picking up the two video tapes, she stood up to leave. He grabbed her hand as she passed him.

'I like it when you bother me, Katrina,' he said softly, holding on tight to her hand. She looked into the seductive blue of his eyes, feeling the familiar tug at her heart. She steeled herself against it and pulled her hand free. She lifted her chin and gave him a haughty look.

'I don't have time for games,' she said loftily. 'I have work to do.'

She heard him laugh as she left the room and she couldn't quite keep from smiling herself.

She did, in actual fact, have work to do: calls to make, lists to check, menus to plan, et cetera. Tonight she was going to have dinner with Sasha and come to a final decision. The Great Decision. Should she or should she not settle on St Barlow and go into business with Sasha growing herbs?

It was exciting and terrifying at the same time.

She settled at her desk, consulting her phone call list and called her brother, who had returned from Europe. The house in London had been sold to an Arab sheikh, Tyler informed her. It was time for her to come to New York to deal with the contents of the mansion, so that they could be put on the market as well.

It was February and the temperatures were way below freezing in New York. Snow lay piled in dirty heaps by the roadsides. The wind came straight from the North Pole. Katrina looked at the sunny sea outside and shivered. 'Do I have to?' she asked.

'No,' he said bluntly. 'I'll get an auction house...'

'OK, OK, I'll come.' She thought of her girlhood room with her great-grandmother's old brass bed in it. Of her mother's paintings, her father's big leather chair. She remembered sitting on his lap in that chair while he read her a story. The stuff memories were made of. It would be unthinkable to have the chair auctioned off, for her mother's paintings to hang in unknown rooms, for strangers to sleep in her bed. The thought was not to be borne.

She called Mary Lou who had finally returned from a lovely skiing weekend. She told Katrina all about it. Katrina listened patiently, as a good friend should. Then she thanked Mary Lou for the video tapes and told her she was coming to New York in a couple of days.

'Great!' said Mary Lou. 'You'll stay here, won't you?'

'You've got my winter clothes.' Mary Lou had offered to store them for her after Katrina had sold the penthouse apartment.

'Right. Let me know when you'll arrive and I'll come and pick you up.'

'Did you check with the library about Max's books? Katrina asked.

There was not a trace of a writer by the name of Max Laurello in the entire New York City library system, Mary Lou told her. 'Maybe he's a fraud,' she offered. 'Maybe it's a cover and he's a spy or a criminal in hiding.'

'Gee, you sure are such an uplifting person, Mary Lou.'

Mary Lou laughed. 'Maybe he uses a pseudonym. Did you ask him?'

'No. I didn't think of it.' And he hadn't told her, either. Maybe this was another one of his little deceptions.

Max did not make an appearance again that afternoon and both of them were out for dinner that night. When Katrina came back from visiting Sasha, she saw the light under Max's office door. He had returned from dinner and was back at work.

She was much too excited to sleep. Over-stimulation was the word: too many thoughts and ideas brewing in her head. She and Sasha had pored over plans and papers and financial projections and the plan to start a business growing hydroponic herbs seemed a viable one. Growing the herbs in water in mesh greenhouses rather than straight in the ground was a way to control insects and diseases. Sasha had done her part of the research, and Katrina had done hers.

Katrina sighed. It was a wonderful feeling finally to have a real goal, something to work towards. Her first priority now was to find a piece of land and start building the greenhouses.

She took a long, relaxing shower, but it did nothing to calm her. If she didn't do something to get her agitated mind diverted to another subject she would lie awake all night thinking about it, or dozing and having visions of forests of parsley or fields of dill waving in the breeze.

What she needed was a cup of camomile tea, which was good for hysteria, sleeplessness, nightmares and stomach upsets. Unfortunately she was out of camomile tea. Now what?

Then it hit her. The films! Doris Day to the rescue!

She pulled on a long silk kimono and went downstairs. She made herself a cup of mint tea—good for the digestion, headaches, dizziness, chills, fever and seasickness, none of which bothered her—and settled herself in front of the VCR and her precious video tapes, each of which contained the pleasures of three films.

Ah, the joy of fantasy! It was so inspiring! Two films and two wedges of mango pie later she still was not sleepy. In fact, she felt quite alive. She poured herself a glass of chardonnay and started film number three. Why not? She did not have to get up in the morning to start a commute into the city to do brain surgery. All she had to do was make sure her herb seedlings got watered.

A while later she heard Max moving around. He came into the sitting-room with a glass in his hand. 'Good God,' he said, 'I thought you'd gone to bed ages ago.'

'I'm not tired,' she said, glancing up at him, feeling her heart doing its little dance of joy again. Her heart seemed to have a life of its own. It loved seeing Max, even if she didn't.

His hair was dishevelled as if he'd been tearing at it. He was wearing rumpled shorts and a faded T-shirt and his eyes looked tired. His precious Isabel had probably worn him out.

Max drank his drink and watched the television—Cary Grant trying to seduce a terrified, virginal Doris Day. Max laughed. 'Scintillating stuff,' he said.

'Oh, go away.'

'I am. I'm going for a swim.'

'Now? In the middle of the night?'

'Why not? I need to unwind or I'll never sleep.'

She knew how that felt. 'Swimming at night is dangerous!'

'No, it's not. I'm not stupid. I'm not going far out.' He put the glass down. 'I won't be long.'

He was back in twenty minutes, quite alive and wearing a short blue cotton bathrobe. His hair was wet, and he looked much refreshed. In fact, he looked vibrant and virile—a man ready for anything. Her heart skipped a beat and she promptly forgot the film. Towering above her stood a real-life man with a rugged face and deep blue eyes, a man who had traversed deserts and jungles and mountains, a man who had kissed her not long ago, a man who threw her off balance and made her heart race. She swallowed hard.

'How was your swim?' she asked for something to say.

'Very relaxing.'

'Have you got Isabel out of your system?'

'I'm afraid she's there to stay,' he said casually, 'but let's not talk about my writing, shall we? I'm off duty, so to speak. Would you care for another drink?'

She was tempted to confront him about the fact that no books by Max Laurello were to be found in all of metropolitan New York, but some instinct told her that this was not the moment.

'Another glass of chardonnay, thanks.'

He went to the bar in the corner of the room and poured them each a drink. He sat down next to her on the sofa, leaned back comfortably and glanced at the television. 'How's Doris doing?'

'She broke out in a rash. She was terrified of Cary Grant making love to her.' Silly woman.

He laughed. 'Now that's what I call romantic.'

She took the remote control and switched the film off. With Max in the room to disturb her heartbeat it was impossible to pay attention to the movie, Cary Grant or no Cary Grant.

'Now why did you do that?'

'I wouldn't want to bore you.'

'I wasn't bored, I was enjoying myself. Turn it on and we'll watch the rest together. I want to know how it ends,' he said, face straight.

'He'll marry her, that's how it ends. That's how they all end.' He was sitting too close. She could smell the sea on his skin. A tiny drop of water dripped from his hair down his temple. She longed to reach out and wipe it away with her hand. She longed to touch him.

'You gave it away,' he said, feigning disappointment. 'You should never give away the ending of a movie. You're a spoilsport.' He reached for the remote control in her hand. Involuntarily she clutched her fingers tightly around it. His hand covered hers. It felt cold from the water. His eyes met hers, amusement lurking in their depths.

'You want to wrestle for it?' he asked softly.

It was a delicious invitation, she had to admit, but so undignified. She let her fingers relax.

'Chicken,' he said. He sat back, not switching on the VCR, his eyes still on her face.

'You're very beautiful,' he commented, 'but I suppose lots of men have told you that.'

'Dozens.'

He nodded. 'I expected so. It's a burden for a woman, isn't it? To be beautiful. My sisters tell me so.'

'I quite enjoy it, actually,' she said. It sure beat the alternative.

'My sisters complain about men only being interested in their bodies.'

'Well, yes, there is that.'

'How do you handle that?'

She held up her now ringless left hand. 'I used to flash my diamond at them and tell them I was married and didn't fool around.'

He nodded. 'For a man on the prowl there's nothing more boring than a virtuous woman. And now? What do you do now?'

'It hasn't been much of a problem here on the island. There aren't many men on the loose.'

'There's me.'

'Are you interested in my body?'

'Hell, no. All I care about is your mind,' he said drily.

'Well, good, then I have nothing to worry about, do I?'

'Not a thing.' He switched the TV on. 'Let's watch the rest of the movie.'

So they did. Cary Grant married Doris Day. He got a rash on their wedding night, but later there was a baby,

just to prove they did make it into bed together in the
end. They never showed anything but a chaste kiss. All
the rest you had to make up in your imagination. Katrina
had no trouble doing it.

She gave a deep sigh when the movie was finished. It
became very quiet in the room. It was very late. Through
the open windows she could hear the sounds of crickets
and other nocturnal creatures celebrating life.

She wanted to celebrate life too. She was feeling well,
she'd gained weight, and Max was sitting next to her.
Max, who kept stirring her soul and body. Max, in
nothing but a terry bathrobe. Max, with his sexy blue
eyes and lips that made her heart sing.

'Is that what you fantasise about?' he asked suddenly.
'A handsome, rich man who bowls you over and marries
you?'

'I don't care if he's handsome or rich. I tried it once,
and it didn't work out.'

'So what do you want? Short, bald and poor?'

'I have no intention of divulging my fantasies to you.'
She yawned eleborately and came to her feet, adjusting
the kimono around her. 'I'm exhausted. I'm going to
bed.'

'Not so fast.' He took her hand and pulled her down
next to him, putting his arms around her and holding
her close to him. 'I thought we both might enjoy the
real thing, rather than fantasy,' he whispered.

'The real thing?' Her heart was doing a somersault.
Fear? Joy? Excitement? All of the above?

'You and me. Here, now.' His voice was soft and seductive. Then he kissed her. She let him. Against all her
better judgement, of course. It was so wonderful, how
could she fight it?

She closed her eyes, aware of the warmth of his body,
the strength of his arms around her, the clean, mas-

culine scent of him. His tongue did tantalising things with hers and her heart beat wildly with excitement.

He lifted his head fractionally. 'How's that?' he whispered.

'I like it,' she whispered back, finding no reason why she should lie.

So he did it some more, and his hands began to wander, stroking her neck, slipping under the kimono and caressing her shoulders with feather-like caresses that made her shiver under his touch. His face moved lower and his lips were warm on her throat. She felt herself grow light and warm and her heart was beating so loudly that she could hear it drum in her ears.

He pushed the kimono aside and his hands cupped her breasts. He sat back a little and gazed at her face, then lowered his eyes to her breasts. 'Beautiful,' he murmured. 'And so soft and warm and lovely.'

The words suffused her body with heat, a tingling sensation like warm spiced wine on a cold night. He lowered his head and his mouth delicately kissed both nipples, one at a time, his tongue stroking and teasing. Oh, such exquisite sensation…such sweet agony! A soft moan escaped her. Her fingers tangled in his hair and her body stirred restlessly against him.

He shifted her gently and nudged her back until she lay on the sofa and she opened her eyes and looked at him.

He was looking at her, his gaze full of hunger and a deep blue fire. His hands were working the sash on her kimono and it fell open, exposing the rest of her body. His hands travelled over her stomach, stroking, as if she was something precious and valuable—a work of art.

'You're beautiful,' he said again, his voice a little rough. His body seemed tense, full of controlled power. 'I want to touch you, get to know every part of you.'

'I thought you weren't interested in my body,' she whispered, her common sense suddenly getting the better of her.

He bent over and his mouth nuzzled her abdomen, a trail of warm, damp kisses. 'I'm not,' he muttered. 'I'm only pretending.'

She laughed softly. 'All right, in that case, don't stop.' Oh, God, what was she doing?

She knew what she was doing. She closed her eyes and his mouth came down on hers, his body pressed up against hers.

Only pretending.

And then there was no more slow, gentle teasing. His kiss was deep and demanding, and a wave of desire washed over her, yet in the midst of the tumultuous demands of her body came again his words.

Only pretending.

A thought occurred to her suddenly and it hit her like a bucket of cold water. All the warmth left her.

He was doing research for his novel. He was using her as Isabel's stand-in, trying to find out what made her tick so that he could use it in his book. It was all just a game to trigger off some inspiration. That was what everything had been all along.

And here she was, accommodating him like a starstruck teenager. She felt cold all over. Her hands gripped his shoulders and she pushed him away, averting her face.

'Play-time's over,' she said, her body rigid.

He sat up, chest heaving. 'What?'

She took in a calming breath. 'I don't want to play any more, that's all.' She struggled into an upright position and closed her kimono. Her hands were shaking.

'What the hell do you mean by that?' His voice was rough with passion and anger.

She took in the hard set of his jaw, her heart hammering. 'I mean just what I said,' she said bravely. 'I don't want to play any more.'

'Who's playing?' he bit out. He came to his feet and towered over her, his eyes a glacial blue. 'Don't worry, sweetheart, I'm not in the habit of forcing myself on women.' He strode to the door. 'All you have to say is no.'

'No,' she said promptly.

She avoided him at breakfast the next morning and went to the orphanage to spend time with the children. She had lunch with Sasha and in the afternoon she began packing for her trip to New York. She wouldn't need to bring much—certainly not her shorts and thin dresses and bikinis.

Max found her packing the small case a while later.

'Where are you going?' he said sharply.

'New York.' To get rid of my childhood, she added silently. And to get rid of you, maybe, came another thought.

'You can't go,' he said imperiously, crossing his arms in front of his chest.

She raised her eyebrows at him. 'Now that's an interesting statement if ever I heard one.' There was faint mockery in her voice, as she intended.

'We have an agreement,' he stated coldly. 'Part of the rental agreement is that you handle my meals and answer the phone.'

'I've made arrangements with Mrs Blackett to stay until after dinner every day I'm gone. She'll cook you dinner and answer the phone.'

'It's not the same.' His voice was hard.

'Not the same as what?'

'As having you around.'

She gave him a mocking look. 'And why would you want me around? Oh, let me guess. To serve as a bit of visual inspiration. Is that it?' The air was charged with tension. Her hands shook.

'And so I can talk to you,' he said tightly.

'Verbal inspiration. Gee, it's starting to sound like quite a job.'

'Well, you were looking for one. I'll pay you.'

'You'll pay me? It's getting more interesting all the time. And what shall I call myself? An inspirational assistant?'

He shrugged. 'Call yourself whatever you want.'

'And what about the physical part of this?'

His jaw went rigid. 'Would you clarify that, please?'

'Not only do you want me for visual and verbal inspiration, you seem to be requiring physical inspiration as well. I'm sorry to disappoint you, but I do not intend to accommodate you.'

There was a pregnant silence. They stared into each other's eyes and she forced herself not to look away.

'I see,' he said at last, his voice cold. 'So that's what that was all about last night.'

She shrugged. 'It took me a while to catch on, sap that I am. I'm merely a stand-in for Isabel. You're just using me.' It sounded so sad, so tragic. She'd let herself get carried away by her own needs, she, a poor love-starved widow, so longing for love and tenderness. It was pathetic.

His face was a mask of anger. His jaws worked. 'I am *using* you?' he asked.

She swallowed and looked straight into the icy blue of his eyes. 'Yes.'

There was a moment of quivering silence. 'By all means,' he said then, his voice heavy with sarcasm, 'don't let me use you.' He walked out, slamming the door.

*   *   *

Figuring out what to do with a mansion full of furniture and artwork was no small matter. So many rooms, so many antiques, so many art objects, so many treasures of all kinds. Once her family had lived here, and many friends had visited, and many servants had kept the place in order. Now all there was was an old caretaker couple, Mr and Mrs Pennybaker, who lived in an apartment above the car garages and made sure the pipes didn't freeze and the mice didn't take possession of the mansion.

Nothing of the old glamour and glitter was evident now. The house was cold and lifeless. The furniture was shrouded in dustcovers. There was the faint smell of mould and dead air. Silence reigned. The place was like a mausoleum. It suited Katrina's mood perfectly.

True to her nature, she made lists. 'THINGS TO SELL'. 'THINGS TO KEEP'. 'THINGS FOR STORAGE'. 'THINGS TO GIVE AWAY'. 'THINGS TO CHECK WITH TYLER'. 'THINGS UNDECIDED'.

It was all more complicated than she'd feared and it was a depressing job. What did you do with thirty-two wonderful paintings your own artist mother had made? Sell them? Put them in storage?

Her mother had died when Katrina was fifteen. There were still days that she missed her terribly. Her mother had had a vivacious, flamboyant personality. She'd not been your standard, run-of-the-mill high-society lady. She hadn't cared much for all the trappings of the rich life, but she and Katrina's father had been madly in love for reasons no one could ever fathom.

Day after day, lists in hand, Katrina moved through the cold, silent rooms and gloom invaded her, taking control of her heart and mind, the way the damp had taken control of the house.

Fortunately, there was Mary Lou, who helped her out on several days and at night dragged her out to attend various pleasurable events. Mary Lou was determined to cheer her up. Katrina was not ready.

She had a meeting with her brother once in his office to discuss money matters, and afterwards they went to dinner and talked about more money matters and all of it was more like a business meeting than a get-together with her own brother and only living blood relative. It was very distressing.

Spending so many long, lonely hours in the mansion gave her a lot of time to think about Max and her confusing feelings for him. But, whatever silly notions and hopes she might nurture, her brain in the end always came up with the same conclusion: self-preservation demanded that she get rid of her infatuation for him or somehow learn to live with it. In a short time she would be back on the island and she'd better come up with a battle plan, some rules, some magic potion.

A week after her arrival, Katrina was sitting on the floor in the middle of her girlhood room, surrounded by her old possessions. It was the only cheerful room in the entire building. Mrs Pennybaker, for some reason, had assumed that Katrina had come to stay at the house and had cleaned and aired the room, made the big brass bed with fresh Pratesi linens, turned up the heat and put a vase of flowers on the dressing-table. The adjoining bathroom had been seen to as well.

From a storage cupboard in the adjoining playroom Katrina had dragged the boxes that contained her childhood toys and spread them around for inspection. She sighed disconsolately. There they were: her Lego blocks, her collection of finger puppets, her innumerable stuffed animals, her dolls, her books. How nice it would be to have a little daughter to give them to!

She might never have a daughter.

She might never have children of any gender for that matter. She was almost twenty-six and practically alone in the world and doomed to stay that way. No man might ever love her for herself, marry her and cherish her.

She was feeling quite sorry for herself. Actually, she was wallowing in it. It was easy to do when you were alone in an empty, mouldy mansion, surrounded by ghosts of the past.

And then there was a sound of heavy footsteps, not the steps of Mr or Mrs Pennybaker, who were both tiny and arthritic and dragged their feet, but the steps of someone big and possibly dangerous. A robber looking for the silver. A perverted killer looking for skinny widows.

She sat perfectly still, forgetting to breathe, her heart pounding wildly against her ribs.

A large, dark shape appeared in the doorway, filling the frame with its bulk. Shiny black dress shoes, sharply pressed trousers, a Burberry trench coat, open to reveal the immaculate suit, the white shirt, the designer tie.

A square-jawed, tanned face. Piercing blue eyes.

Max Laurello, all dressed up.

CHAPTER SIX

NOT a burglar, not a perverted killer. Max. Her heart changed its panicked rhythm into something a bit less frantic. Not that it calmed down, of course. Her heart was never calm with him around. Her body began to shake. She tightened her arms around the life-size baby doll she'd been clutching against her breast.

He looked magnificent. He'd had a haircut, and his angular face seemed more commanding than ever with its square chin and piercing blue eyes. In his city clothes he looked like a sophisticated man of the world. He might be at home in jungles and deserts and on tiny Caribbean islands, but he certainly looked at home in New York City as well.

His mouth opened, then closed as his gaze settled on the doll in her arms. An odd look came into his eyes.

She took a steadying breath, finding her tongue. 'What the hell are you doing here?' she demanded, tossing the doll unceremoniously aside. 'You nearly gave me a heart attack! How did you get in here, anyway?'

'It's a doll,' he said incongruously.

'What did you think it was?'

His eyes were inscrutable. 'A baby. The way you were sitting there it looked real.'

'Well, it wasn't,' she snapped, 'and you didn't answer my question. How did you get in the house?'

His mouth curved. 'A tiny little grandma let me in. She appeared to have a problem walking, so I suggested she tell me where you were and I'd find my own way.'

'How did you get past the gate? Wasn't anybody there?'

'Oh, yes,' he said drily, 'somebody was there. A huge gorilla of a man with a fancy uniform and a gun. But he was sleeping like a baby and it seemed a shame to wake him up. The gate was open.'

Katrina sighed. You couldn't count on anybody any more these days. She only hoped the burglar alarm system was functioning properly. The guard who came at night probably was a college student who slept the night away. She sighed. Problems, problems. She'd be happy to have all this taken care of so that she could go back to St Barlow where she could leave her door and windows open day and night.

'Quite a palace, this,' said Max.

'My ancestral home,' she said loftily. 'Generations have lived here.' Well, four, her own included. Not exactly a medieval Scottish castle, but by American standards not half bad.

She scrambled off the floor and sat down on the edge of the brass bed. She couldn't help staring at him. He looked very imposing in his expensive suit, the white shirt contrasting so deeply with his tan, his silk tie knotted so perfectly. He looked drop-dead gorgeous. And the fact that she knew what lay beneath the clothes—the broad chest, the hard, flat plane of his stomach, the muscular legs—made her heart ache with painful longing. She noticed the faint smell of his aftershave, familiar yet strange now that he was dressed so differently.

He wasn't supposed to be here. What was he doing here in New York?

'What are you doing here?' she asked, hearing the ambivalence in her own voice. One part of her was jubilant to see him, the other in shock. She'd thought him safely ensconced on the island and now he was here. The shock of it was beginning to sink in. She had wanted to be away from him. A relationship with him was too complicated and too stressful. She'd had it with complicated and stressful relationships. What she wanted was simple and easy: I love him and he loves me, all the time and forever. Was it asking too much?

Of course it was. Even she, in her heart of hearts, knew that. But why not dream the impossible? Why not hope for a miracle?

He shrugged out of his coat and tossed it on to a chair. 'I had to do an interview and I had to see my publisher in New York. I thought I'd look you up.'

She didn't buy it. She'd left only a week ago, and he'd never uttered a word about any interview or publisher. She looked at him dubiously, remaining eloquently silent. Somehow she had to get rid of him. She didn't want him here, in the house of her childhood, while she was doing away with her past. It was too much to handle all at once.

'What exactly are you doing?' he asked.

'I'm disposing of my past and my possessions, so to speak. My brother and I are selling the house and I'm trying to figure out what to do with all the furniture and artwork and other stuff.'

'How about a tour of the place?' he suggested.

'No.' She glanced at her watch. 'I have some real-estate people coming over. Besides, you're just doing research and I don't want my background ending up in your book.'

His jaw clenched and his eyes darkened. 'What the hell is the matter with you, Katrina?'

She gave him a wide-eyed look. 'Nothing. I'm on to you, that's all.'

'Can't I say or do anything without you assuming that I have ulterior motives?'

'No,' she said coldly. 'And if you'll excuse me I'm busy.' She stared right into his eyes, willing herself not to feel his magnetism, the pulling on her senses. She could not afford to get involved with him. Oh, such brave thoughts! Such courageous decisions! It was all so much easier when he wasn't around to divert her from her grand resolutions. Here he stood, all male virility, looking at her with those brilliant blue eyes, and she felt weak as soft butter. All she wanted was to throw herself into his arms and have him kiss her senseless.

'How about dinner tonight?' he asked.

'No,' she said, hanging on to her common sense for dear life. She could not allow herself to self-destruct.

His eyes narrowed. 'Why are you doing this? What's wrong with my having a look at this house? With the two of us going out together? What are you afraid of, Katrina? That you might be in love with me?'

Well, there it was, out in the open. Not that she would admit it, of course. Not in a million years. She gave him a mocking smile. 'You have quite an ego, don't you?'

She saw the anger leap into his eyes. He came towards the bed, took her by the arms and lifted her unceremoniously to her feet. 'Now you listen to me! I've just about had it with this ridiculous behaviour of yours, do you understand?'

His outburst threw her off-guard and her heart leaped into her throat. 'Get your hands off me!' she said in the voice of an outraged virgin.

'No,' he said, 'I will not. I had hoped you had come to your senses after that outrageous scene the night before you left the island,' Max went on, looking straight into her eyes. His face was very close, all hard angles and cool determination. His chin jutted dangerously. 'Let me make something clear to you, Katrina. Not all my conversations and actions are necessarily geared to accommodate my work. I am a writer, yes, and I'll take my inspiration wherever I can find it. However, I am also a man living and experiencing life the way most people do. When I show an interest in this house, for example, it might just be that I am interested in the house because it is the place where you grew up, and you, Katrina, are a person in my life I find interesting for various reasons, not all related to Isabel.'

'I'm so flattered,' she said, shaking his hands away from her arms and backing away from him.

'Don't act like a spoiled brat.' He pushed his jacket aside and put his hands into his pockets. 'Now,' he went on, 'shall we start over? I'd like to see the house. How about a tour?'

There was a variety of unkind things she wanted to say to him, but none very intelligent. Fortunately she had the presence of mind and enough self-respect to keep them to herself. She gathered what shreds of dignity she had left and straightened her shoulders.

'As I said, I have some real-estate people coming any minute. It's not possible now.' It was even the honest-to-God truth.

'How about tomorrow?'

'I might be able to work you in tomorrow afternoon, late,' she said generously.

'Excellent.' He turned on his heels, picked up his coat from the chair and marched out of the room.

'You shouldn't have told him where I was!' Katrina wailed at Mary Lou that night. 'Or at least you could have called me and asked!'

Mary Lou, resplendent in a designer lounging outfit with a tiger-stripe design, looked penitent. She did it well with her big brown eyes. 'I know, I know, but the caterers were here and I was busy and I didn't give it much thought. I just told him your address, and I *was* going to call you, but then I got distracted.' She gave Katrina a pensive look. 'Why didn't you tell me just how gorgeous he is?'

'It didn't seem to matter.'

'It *always* matters, one way or another.' She tossed her long blonde curls carelessly over her shoulders. 'Oh, guess who called today? Stefan! He's back from Rome. I invited him to the party. He's dying to see you, he said.'

So they talked about the party, which Mary Lou was having for her, Katrina. She'd see her friends again, meet some new people. She was looking forward to it.

Katrina forgave Mary Lou her transgression. After all, who was perfect?

The next morning, at the ungodly hour of eight forty-five, Mary Lou awakened her rudely by practically crashing through her bedroom door and turning on the television set.

'It's him!' she yelled. 'Look!'

Katrina hoisted herself in a semi-sitting position and peered bleary-eyed at the huge screen—only the biggest and the best for the guests at the Valentine residence.

It was him all right. Max Laurello, larger than life, blue-eyed and full of charm on a breakfast show.

Katrina was instantly awake, her heart pumping blood and oxygen to her brain at record speed.

Max was obviously talking about his fourth book, now out on the shelves, but she only heard the last few sentences of the interview, including a reference to an upcoming movie. A picture of the book cover was flashed on the screen: *In Pursuit of Baby Black* by Max Killain.

Max Killain. Her heart turned over in her chest. 'Oh, my God,' she croaked, 'he's Max Killain!'

Mary Lou switched the set off. Katrina stared at Mary Lou, stupefied. Mary Lou stared at Katrina, equally stupefied.

'I can't believe it's him,' Mary Lou said, her voice low and awestruck. She looked like a wild woman with her hair standing out in all directions and her silk kimono hanging half-open. 'Didn't he used to be a photo-journalist before he started writing novels?'

Katrina nodded. 'Yes. He told me about that.'

'But he never told you he was Killain?'

'No.' Katrina took a pillow and clutched it to her chest. She needed something to hold on to.

Mary Lou sagged down on the side of the bed. 'Good God, Katrina, the man is famous! All his books make the bestseller list! They're making a movie of the one that's just coming out!' She frowned suddenly. 'If he hadn't come to see me here yesterday to ask about you, I wouldn't have recognised him. I wonder why he didn't tell you?'

So did Katrina.

Mary Lou, however, didn't wonder long. Her face lit up as an idea struck her. 'We must invite him to the party tonight! It's perfect! Stefan will be here and the Roxburghs and Sarina, and Cassandra and Jean-Paul. I bet he'd love to talk to Cassandra. Did you read her latest opus? I'll——'

'He won't come,' said Katrina. 'He's not the kind that enjoys being the showpiece of the evening.'

'Well, we can try. It's a little last-minute, of course, but...'

'I don't want him here.'

Mary Lou stared at her. 'It's only a small party—I've only invited our closest friends.'

'You're giving this party for me, you said, and I don't want you to invite him, Mary Lou.'

'Why not?'

'I don't want him around! You know that! I've bared my soul to you about him and now you want to invite him to your house! I thought you understood what I'd been telling you!'

'I didn't know you were talking about Max Killain!'

'What difference does it make? He's still the same man!'

Mary Lou shook her head decisively. 'No, he's not. It makes all the difference in the world. He's Max Killain, writer of bestsellers, not some flunky writer living on the fringes.'

'God, you're such a snob, Mary Lou.'

Mary Lou came to her feet and put her hands on her hips. 'You can't possibly deny us and our friends the opportunity to get closer acquainted with Max Killain! Don't be so selfish, Katrina!'

Katrina wondered who was the selfish one, but refrained from uttering the question. There was, however, the issue of Mary Lou putting on this party for her, spending time and money to get their friends together as well as a few interesting new people for her to meet. Max Killain would make quite a hit.

If he came.

Which he wouldn't.

No doubt he had plans for the evening already, and if not he'd come up with an excuse.

Katrina waved her hand in dismissal. 'Oh, go ahead, invite him.'

Fortunately, she had all day to get used to the idea of Max Laurello being the famous writer Max Killain. By the time he showed up at the house for his tour, she felt she could handle the situation.

'I saw your interview on TV this morning,' she told him, 'at least the last couple of minutes of it. Congratulations.'

'Thank you,' he said evenly.

'I've read your books and I'm very impressed.'

His mouth turned down. 'I was afraid of that.'

This was not the kind of answer Katrina had anticipated. 'Don't you like me being impressed?'

'No,' he said.

'Why not? Doesn't everybody like his or her ego stroked?'

'There's only so much stroking I can take before it gets really boring. Also, the people doing the most stroking always want something from me.'

'Yes, of course.' Having dwelt among the rich and famous and having jetted with the jet-set, she knew he was right. 'Well, rest assured that I don't want anything from you,' she said coldly.

He gave an amused smile, then touched his finger to her cheek in an unexpected tender gesture. 'That's what I like about you, Katrina. You want nothing from me.'

Her heart turned over. His eyes were hypnotising her and she tore her gaze away and stepped back from him.

'Why didn't you tell me who you were?' she demanded.

'You would have been so impressed,' he said drily.

'Hah!' She'd dined with royalty, played tennis with Hollywood stars, partied with celebrities. She, impressed with meeting Max Killain? Oh, come on!

Well, she would have been, to a degree. After all, she much respected the written word, especially when arranged into novels of great entertainment.

He ignored her sneer. 'And I'd had enough of women who were impressed with me,' he went on. 'Not a moment's peace.'

'Life is hell,' she commiserated. 'Especially for the rich and famous. I'm actually quite happy to be poor.' It was a lie, of course, but it sounded virtuous. Not that he bought it for a moment.

He rolled his eyes. 'Now let's have the tour of the palace, Princess.'

A few days ago, in anticipation of the visits of real-estate agents, estate auction appraisers, art experts and various other *cognoscenti*, the dustcovers had all been removed. A team of cleaners had come in to sweep and scrub and dust and polish and buff. Everything sparkled and gleamed with regal grandeur. However, a homey atmosphere was lacking.

They went down the wide, curving staircase and started at the first floor with its many vast rooms—the sitting-room, the library, the study, the music-room, the morning-room, the dining-room, the sun-room, and so forth.

'It's difficult to believe you grew up here,' Max said, taking in the antique furniture, the velvet draperies, the glittering chandeliers, the priceless oriental carpets.

'Why?'

'You don't seem to fit in with all this.'

'Why not?'

'I'm not sure.'

They moved from room to room, and she told him about her childhood, about her artist mother, about her brother trying to save the family business. She showed him her mother's paintings, took him to her favourite hiding places, and showed him where she had secretly carved her name on the bottom of an eighteenth-century chair worth thousands.

'Don't you mind selling the house?' he asked.

She considered this for a moment. 'I don't care as much as I thought I would. It's only a house. And besides, it's a big, pretentious, pompous kind of a house. And the furniture—it belongs in a museum. It isn't even comfortable. It's all for show.'

He smiled, saying nothing.

'Don't you agree?'

'Actually, yes.' There was humour in his eyes. 'That's why you don't seem to fit in. You're not a pretentious, pompous kind of person.'

'It's my mother's fault. She never was very impressed with all this. She was very much her own person. She loved cooking and pottering around in the kitchen, driving the staff crazy. She didn't fit in very well, either.'

The tour over, they went back to her old bedroom where Max had left his coat. The room was still the way she had left it at the age of nineteen, except for the boxes of her toys now sitting in the middle of the floor.

'And this was your room?' he asked.

'Yes, until I was nineteen.' It was more than a room, it was a suite, actually—a bedroom, a dressing-room, a bathroom and a separate playroom for her toys.

'Didn't you go away to college?'

'I went to Columbia and I lived at home for the first year. Then I got married and lived in the city. I finished college while I was married.'

'You've never lived on your own, then?'

'I lived plenty on my own.'

Her words hung in the silence. She saw his gaze move from her face to her hands. She realised they were clenched into fists and she hid them behind her back. Too late, of course.

'Why did you get married?' he asked then.

'Because my father asked me to. He married me off, so to speak.'

His eyes narrowed. 'Married you off?'

'It was some sort of business deal.'

'And you let that happen to yourself?' There was outrage in his voice.

She shrugged casually. 'Hey, it was a girl's dream. He wanted me to marry *Bastian MacKenzie*. Just imagine!'

How stupid she had been, how infatuated, how totally lacking in common sense. She couldn't bear to think about it. It hadn't been all her father's doing. She'd been equally responsible for the whole sordid business.

'Bastian MacKenzie?' Max asked incredulously. 'You were married to that worthless playboy? I didn't know he had a wife.'

'Don't feel bad. He had trouble remembering himself.'

Again there was a silence while he looked at her intently. 'Oh, my God,' he whispered.

'Please don't tell me how sorry you are for me. I came away relatively unscathed—body and soul. My body may be on the thin side, but I am in excellent health, and my soul is tough as old leather.'

He threw back his head and laughed heartily. Then his eyes met hers and his face relaxed in a smile.

'I've missed you,' he said. He reached for her hand and drew her towards him. Then he lifted her chin with a finger and touched her mouth with his.

She was instantly aflame. It was awful. It was frightening. Every time he touched her she responded automatically. She couldn't stand herself! How could she be so spineless? So stupid? If she didn't want him, why then did she enjoy his kissing her so much?

She wanted to put her arms around him and kiss him back, but a small remnant of pride rescued her from her folly and she drew back.

Their eyes met and held. She could hear her heart pumping in the silence. The smile had left his face. His eyes were dark, his expression inscrutable. He released her slowly.

'When are you coming back?' he asked.

She took a few steps away from him and shrugged. 'Maybe I'm not.' Shame on her. She was just saying that to annoy him. Of course she was coming back. She was going to start a business and grow herbs on St Barlow. She wanted warmth and sunshine and sea breezes and fresh air. She was sick and tired of the cold and the wet.

His expression gave nothing away. 'How about dinner tonight?' he suggested.

'I can't. Mary Lou is having a party for me tonight.' She felt a sinking sense of inevitability. 'She asked me to invite you. She saw you on TV this morning.' She paused meaningfully. 'She's *extremely* impressed. If you come, you're going to be the showpiece of the evening. There'll be lots of other women who'll also be very impressed.' If that wouldn't turn him off, nothing would.

'Tell her I'll be delighted to come,' he said, face impassive.

Katrina stood in front of the big wardrobe that housed her clothes, trying to decide what to wear for the party. She was not in a good frame of mind. She felt thwarted and used and she did not delight in these emotions. She was fighting the impulse to slip out of the door and escape the party.

However, the party was for her, and she was looking forward to seeing her friends. She *wanted* to enjoy herself. She took a deep breath. Well, then she *would* enjoy herself, plain and simple. All she had to do was ignore Max.

Yeah, sure. No problem. She grimaced and surveyed the colourful collection of silks and velvets and satins. So, what to wear? The long bronze silk? No, too serious, too formal. The low-cut black velvet? No, too unimaginative. She wanted something light and fluffy, something playful to cheer her up. Something with a little pizzazz, a touch of dazzle. She extracted a raspberry mini, a deliciously flirty thing that hugged her body in all the right places, then flared out into a flouncy little skirt layered with black. Perfect!

She slipped the dress on, put on some long, sexy earrings and batted her lashes at herself in the mirror, feeling better already.

The buffet table was a feast for the eyes, not to speak of the stomach. In the centre sparkled an ice sculpture of a mama kangaroo, the pouch containing an opened can of Beluga caviare. Mary Lou had an off-centre sense of humour; not for her sculptures of swans or lotus flowers. Silver platters and crystal bowls full of the most exquisite delicacies graced the table—smoked salmon, pâté de foie gras, marinated wild mushrooms, *terrine de poisson*. French champagne flowed and sparkled, as did Russian vodka and Scotch whisky and Barbadian rum.

The guests were equally illustrious and hailed from various parts of the globe. Diamonds glittered and sparkled, as did the conversation. Sometimes, anyway. Everyone was most delighted to find Max Killain present, especially the females, who all were *very* impressed and vied for his attention. Katrina watched as she ate caviare and slowly sipped a vodka on ice.

Sarina, a delicate Italian Contessa, was the lucky one for the moment. Max looked magnificent in his evening clothes. Tall, commanding, handsome. He looked aloof, the strong, silent type that women loved to draw out. They were all trying to draw him out. As far as Katrina could tell, none of them was very successful. Max remained politely distant, smiling a faint, polite smile, looking more and more intriguing.

Katrina scooped some more caviare out of the kangaroo's pouch and ate it, half listening to the man beside her extolling the virtues of mud baths. She managed to disengage herself and strolled casually over to Max and the Contessa.

'Hello, Max,' she said. 'Nice interview this morning. I can't wait for your next book to be finished.'

His eyes met hers and it was quite clear that he knew exactly what she meant. Of course he did; he was a smart man. Had he not, she'd have been very disappointed in him.

Miracle of miracles, his cool face warmed in a smile. 'Hello, Katrina,' he said. 'Have you met Sarina?'

'We've met,' said Katrina, smiling sweetly at the Contessa. She smiled back at Katrina, equally sweet. Then she floated off, apparently having decided her luck had run out for the moment.

Several people joined them and conversation ensued. Momentarily distracted, Katrina noticed a rather flamboyant couple enter the room, she in a slinky gown of shimmering emerald-green silk, he in a night-blue velvet evening suit with a bow-tie to match. She had a shock of black curls, he a greying ponytail hanging halfway down his back.

The woman looked familiar. Katrina searched her memory and it produced the answer: Cassandra Marble, famous author of international glitz novels set in New York, Hollywood, London, Paris, Rome, Rio, Hong Kong and other hotbeds of decadent living.

Cassandra glanced around the room, surveying the guests. Katrina felt a sudden, odd sensation and, glancing up at Max, saw him staring at the woman, stony-faced. She looked back at Cassandra, whose eyes had settled on Max. The woman smiled suddenly, and in a rustle of silk she came breezing over towards them, the ponytail man in velvet right behind her.

'Max!' she said, her voice soft and melodious. 'How delightful to find you here!' She kissed the air by his cheek, first right, then left, then right again, a European fad that seemed not to fade.

'Hello, Cassandra.' Max's voice was cool, his face devoid of expression. The air suddenly crackled with tension. Katrina's stomach clenched. She glanced at the smiling Cassandra, then back at Max's emotionless face. Something was going on here.

'Have you met?' came Mary Lou's voice. There followed a flurry of introductions all round. Cassandra was tall and she smiled down at Katrina as she shook her hand, her green eyes observing her intently, calculating, considering.

Katrina took an instant dislike to her, an instinctive reaction, a gut feeling that Cassandra was trouble. People started talking. Katrina listened and observed.

Cassandra and Max had known each other for a long time, it appeared. They had the same publisher, the same agent and the same taste for travel, albeit that Cassandra enjoyed luxury hotels while Max preferred to camp out with nomads.

The man's name was Jean-Paul Papadopoulos. He was a famous European interior designer, half-French, half-Greek. Cassandra had commissioned JPP, as she called him, to redecorate her New York penthouse apartment as well as her villa in the south of France.

'It's going to be exquisite,' she said. 'You must all come and see when it's finished. I'll have a party. I'll send you an invitation.'

Katrina could hardly wait.

Cassandra kept on talking. She was reminiscing, looking meaningfully at Max. St Moritz, skiing, a party. Katrina knew this particular party game, yet she couldn't rid herself of the tight feeling in her chest, a feeling she was intimately familiar with. A feeling she had absolutely no intention of feeling, only she was. She was about to leave the group of rapt listeners when Max's hand lightly touched her shoulder. With a few polite words, he excused the two of them and led her away to the bar where they both got another drink.

'That must have been quite an affair you had with her,' Katrina said casually. It was none of her business, of course, but she couldn't help herself. She couldn't help feeling the heaviness in her chest. It had no business being there.

He ignored her remark and tossed back a large swallow of whisky. Conrad, Mary Lou's husband, came up to the bar and started a conversation with Max, giving Katrina the opportunity to escape. She mingled, she talked, she laughed. She kept looking at Max, who seemed forever surrounded by women gazing up at him adoringly. She was standing at the buffet table with Jean-Paul Papadopoulos, sampling the food, when she noticed Cassandra talking to Max again. JPP noticed too and his face took on an expression of melancholy sadness. He glanced back at Katrina and gave her a dejected smile.

'I think she has not forgotten him,' he said, resignation in his voice. He scooped some caviare out of the kangaroo's pouch. 'She is always...' he frowned '...how do you say? Pining? Always pining for him.'

Her stomach clenched tight. She couldn't swallow the smoked salmon in her mouth. She was going to choke to death. She took a gulp of vodka and forced the salmon down. Her legs were shaky and her head felt foggy. She stared blindly at the dripping kangaroo. This was absurd. She was letting her emotions run away with her. She took a deep breath and collected herself. She was good at collecting herself; she'd had lots of experience.

So she smiled and charmed her way through the next hour, talking to old friends. She knew most of the people at the party and it was easy enough to have a little innocent fun. And what was wrong with Stefan, who was an old friend, putting his arm lightly around her as they both stood in front of the mantelpiece examining an ornate marble and brass and ivory elephant clock? It was a masterpiece of kitsch as far as Katrina was concerned. It was, in actual fact, a priceless antique treasure, of which she was well aware, owning a mansion full of items of similar noble distinction.

Stefan was playfully nibbling at her ear, whispering something not very profound about old times and new beginnings. Stefan imagined himself a real charmer. She would not, normally, have let him get away with nibbling at her ear, and, no matter what the old times, she was not interested in new times with Stefan.

Max loomed over them the next minute. Claiming her hand, he swiftly extracted her from Stefan's arm in a gesture of undisputable authority.

'If you'll excuse me,' he said coolly, giving Stefan a look that would have shrivelled an emperor. He led her out of the room to the large marble-floored foyer.

She shook his arm away from her shoulder. 'What's that all about?' she asked, feeling tense with anger at his autocratic manner.

'I didn't think you'd appreciate being pawed over by that lover boy,' he said curtly.

He was right, of course, but she would never admit it.

She gave him a haughty look. 'Actually, I was quite enjoying it. Stefan is an old friend, and I didn't need any rescuing.'

His jaw went rigid and his eyes blazed straight into hers. 'What kind of silly game are you playing, Katrina?'

'I have no idea what you mean,' she said with a light shrug. 'I'm merely enjoying the party and talking to old friends. Just as you are.'

'I'm not pawing or being pawed!' he said with barely constrained fury.

This was true, technically. She crossed her arms in front of her chest and took on a casual pose. 'Physically speaking, no, but verbally and visually there's plenty of pawing going on between you and assorted females. So don't give me that "holier than thou" routine!'

His jaws were clamped together and he stared at her without saying a word. Then he took her arm. 'Just stay with me,' he said between clenched teeth.

'You make me feel so wanted,' she said sweetly, but he ignored her as he led her back into the room.

Being held so close certainly was not an unpleasant physical sensation, yet her mind was not having a good time. Having her by his side didn't keep the other women away. Truly, they were vultures. She didn't like what was going on. She couldn't wait for people to start leaving, most especially the Contessa and Cassandra who had been haunting Max all night.

It was disgusting. How cheap to throw yourself like that at a man! Had they no self-respect? Apparently not.

And how pitiful to get herself so worked up about this. She must be in love. Or neurotic. Or both.

She looked at Max next to her, his square jaw, his blue, blue eyes, and her heart contracted painfully. A sure sign of love.

She was in love. She was jealous. She was neurotic. She was terrified. The last thing she needed after Bastian was a love-affair doomed for disaster.

She was caught in the grip of kamikaze madness.

Oh, God, what was she going to do?

CHAPTER SEVEN

KATRINA felt a hand lightly touching her arm and she glanced up into a pair of glittering green eyes. 'It just occurred to me who you are!' said Cassandra, looking triumphant. 'Bastian MacKenzie was your husband, wasn't he?'

'It's hard to remember,' said Katrina, looking vague.

'Oh, darling, we must do lunch some time!'

Katrina groaned inwardly. No worse nightmare could she envision. Another author looking for inspiration. She could already imagine herself and Bastian in one of Cassandra's torrid novels. Then again, perhaps she should look at this as an opportunity: make a career of being inspirational assistant to famous authors.

When hell freezes over, she said to herself. Stay with the parsley. Next to her, Max remained silent and aloof.

'I'd love to have lunch,' she said with a cheery smile, 'but I'm quite booked up these days. I'm in the midst of selling my house here in New York and disposing of the artwork and the antiques. The place is too monstrous and I can't be bothered managing it.' It sounded good. A lot better than saying that selling it was an act of desperation in order to rescue the ailing family business.

Jean-Paul's lean face began to glow with sudden interest. 'Antiques?' he enquired. 'You are selling your antiques?'

'A mansion full of them,' she said irreverently. It was much easier to treat it lightly rather than make a big drama out of it and, God forbid, evoke their pity.

It so happened that Jean-Paul was looking for some choice antiques to add culture and sophistication to some of the abodes he was decorating for several of his American clients. One thing led to another, and the end of it was that Katrina found herself promising him a tour of the house the next day to see if there might be anything of interest there. She rather liked his Continental charm and why not give him the opportunity?

Cassandra smiled at Katrina. 'I met your husband once. In Paris, last year. A very interesting man.' She turned to Max. 'Did you know Bastian?'

'No,' Max replied tersely.

Katrina tensed, aware of the weight of his arm around her shoulders.

'Where did you two meet?' Cassandra looked so friendly, so interested. 'In New York?'

He shook his head. 'Abroad,' he said vaguely.

Again, Cassandra smiled at Katrina. 'I really would like to do lunch. Do call me if you find yourself with some time, all right?'

Katrina smiled back. 'I'll try,' she said, lying through her teeth. It was all so civilised, so hypocritical. She wanted to scream.

When finally most of the guests had left, Max took her into the library off the large entrance hall and closed the door behind them.

'What do you want?' she asked, feeling tense and uneasy.

In answer, he took her in his arms and kissed her. She felt the heat of his mouth invade her, and she pushed herself away from him, hands braced against his chest. 'Why can't you just leave me alone?'

'I don't want to,' he said.

'But *I* do! I don't want to be involved with you.'

He pushed his hands in his pockets and looked at her levelly. 'You *are* involved with me, Katrina. We share a house on St Barlow, we have an agreement, we interact on a daily basis.'

True. Unfortunately. She scowled at him. 'That doesn't mean I should have a romp in bed with you, which is what you're after.'

His mouth quirked. 'You make it sound so... tawdry, so vulgar.'

'Mindless copulation often is,' she said theatrically.

'Do you think that's what it would be?'

She shrugged indifferently. 'I don't see what else.'

He leaned a little closer. 'Oh, yes, you do see, Katrina,' he said softly, and the dark, suggestive look in his eyes made warmth rush to her face. Damn the man!

She rallied all her powers of self-control and gave him a cool, disdainful look. Well, she tried. 'If you want a bed partner, go ask Cassandra,' she suggested. 'She'll be more than willing to go back with you to your hotel. She'll dump Jean-Paul in a flash. Or ask Sarina, or any of the others, but do me a favour and stay away from me.'

He cocked a brow. 'Don't tell me you're jealous,' he said levelly.

Jealous.

Suddenly it was all too much. There was a welling-up of emotion—she could feel it rush through her, a hot wave of anger and anguish, unstoppable, washing away everything in its path. It was terrifying. Her legs trembled and her throat closed. It was coming from somewhere deep inside her, a dark hiding place full of buried memories and secret emotions—the legacy of an unfaithful husband and an unhappy marriage.

He frowned. 'Katrina? What's wrong?'

She couldn't speak. Tears filled her eyes and to her horror she began to cry.

He reached out to her and she backed away. 'Leave me alone!' Her voice was thick with tears. 'I am sick and tired of men like you and women like Cassandra and Sarina!' She clenched her hands into fists, and the tears kept running down her cheeks and it was like being transported back into the past. She remembered facing Bastian, saying the same things. 'They can have you! All of them!'

'I don't want them,' he said calmly. 'I want you.' And then he was kissing her again, his mouth capturing hers as if he owned it.

It was not the gentle, sensuous kiss of a romantic lover. It was a kiss that marked territory and claimed possession. A kiss that said, You're mine whether you like it or not. A kiss that should infuriate her because of its macho pretensions and arrogant demands.

Instead it totally overwhelmed her. It made her blood sing and her head spin. How wonderful to be kissed like this! To feel his strong arms around her, his warm mouth conquering hers with so much determination. Here was a man who knew what he wanted, and it was her. She wanted to believe it. She *needed* to believe it.

Oh, God. What was happening to her? How could she be so weak? So without backbone? Giving in to him was nothing short of digging her own grave, figuratively speaking.

The kiss changed, becoming more gentle, more sensuous, and a dizzy desire took hold of her. He pressed her closer against him and her body sang to his touch. She began to tremble and she couldn't feel the ground under her feet any more.

He released her suddenly, leaving her reeling and light-headed. His eyes were a dark, inky blue and he gave her a long silent look. The air quivered with tension.

'Cassandra was a bad mistake,' he said slowly, 'but it was eight years ago. I do not like to run into her because she irritates the hell out of me and I don't like being reminded of my own stupidity.'

Katrina said nothing.

He turned abruptly and walked out of the room.

Well, she had to admit, it was nice to be wanted, and Max said he wanted her. She lay in bed, too restless to sleep. Max's words kept repeating themselves in her head.

'I don't want them ... I want you.'

Bastian too had been surrounded by glamorous women who were after him for whatever they could get out of him, and he had happily obliged them. He had never come home to her and said, Sweetheart, you are my one and only love, and all these women leave me absolutely cold. All I want is you. She had dreamed of that, of course. In the beginning anyway, until she had realised that her marriage was a farce and Bastian had no intention of being a husband in the traditional sense of the word.

Max said he wanted her. He said Cassandra had been a bad mistake. Everybody made mistakes. She had made some very bad ones herself.

She turned her face into the pillow and sighed. She wanted so very much to believe him. She wanted so very much to be loved by him, to be his one and only woman.

She wanted so very much to believe in fairy-tales.

The next afternoon Jean-Paul Papadopoulos arrived at the mansion with Cassandra in tow. Katrina had not expected to see Cassandra, but there wasn't much she could do about it. Cassandra smiled. Katrina smiled. All was very nice and civilised on the surface.

Although both Cassandra and JPP examined the furniture and artwork with poker faces, making polite and professional comments only, it was clear enough to Katrina, who knew how to read the faces of those trying to hide their feelings, that they were quite aware of having stumbled on to a veritable treasure of valuable furniture. Deals might be made here! Bargains to obtain!

Oh, yes, Katrina knew what they were thinking. She was sorry now she'd invited Jean-Paul to come.

Max showed up minutes after they had departed to consult and conspire about possible purchases: the French oak coffee-table, her parents' antique bed.

She wasn't surprised to see Max; she knew he wasn't going to leave her alone. He wasn't a man who gave up easily. She felt her heart make its familiar little leap at the sight of him.

'How about some dinner?' he asked.

'No. I'm going to stay here and finish my room.' She did not want to go out with him. She felt too fragile and she didn't trust herself. She stared out of the window into the wintry darkness, at the frigid, ghostly gardens, the stone-cold grey city buildings. Even the lights had no warmth in them. A lead sky hung overhead, heavy with pollution, obscuring stars and moon.

'What do you have to do?' he asked.

'I'm going to take most of my toys back with me to the orphanage and I'll need to pack them up, and what I want to keep I'll get ready for storage. Mrs Pennybaker will make me some soup and a sandwich.'

'I'll order us food in.'

She waved her hand. 'Whatever.'

He came towards her and put his hands on her arms. 'What's wrong?' he asked quietly.

'Nothing's wrong!' Then, to her mortification, she burst into tears.

'They want my parents' bed,' she sobbed. 'Imagine! Cassandra and her sleazy lovers in my parents' bed!'

'I'd rather not,' he said drily.

She tried to pull away, but he held her firmly against him. She smelled the clean manly scent of him, felt the soft, smooth fabric of his shirt against her cheek, the warmth of his body underneath. It felt so good, so comforting. Her body relaxed against him.

'Don't sell the bed,' he said, 'if it upsets you.'

'I don't want the bed. I've got my own. I just don't want Cassandra to have it. I didn't know Jean-Paul was going to bring her along.'

'Then don't sell it to her. Forget selling any of it to private individuals or antique dealers. It's not worth the hassle and the emotions. Let Christie's handle it all.'

She took a deep breath, trying to control herself. 'That's what I'm going to do. It was stupid of me to let them in here. I did it for Jean-Paul. He seemed like a nice guy.' A small sob escaped her. 'I'll be glad when all this is over. I hate it, I hate it.' She began to cry again.

He handed her a big white handkerchief and she wiped ineffectually at her eyes, smearing eyeshadow and mascara all over everything, no doubt. The tears kept coming.

'I don't have any place to go home to any more,' she whimpered.

'You have your brother.'

'I know, but—but he ... we—we're more like friendly acquaintances than family. He's single and he has an apartment, but he's never there. It's not the same.' She was feeling sorry for herself. Poor Katrina all alone in the big bad world. 'I feel so alone,' she said shakily, and the tears kept on coming and it felt good to just let them go. 'I've got nobody.'

'You've got me.'

She lifted her face to him. 'You? How's that?'

'Well, I'm here now, holding you and comforting you, and I've rented part of your house on the island and, since I'll be writing books for a long time to come, I'll be there for a long time to come. In other words, you're not alone, you've got me.'

She felt the solid beat of his heart under her cheek. 'All you need is one more female in your life and they can put you in a padded room. Those were your words.'

'But you're different. Now, let's go out to dinner. Tomorrow night I'll help you pack up your things in here.'

'I'm not hungry,' she said.

'You're always hungry. Come on.' His voice brooked no argument. He moved into action—took her coat, put it on her, handed her her handbag and pushed her out of the door. He led her down the curving staircase, out of the front door and into the waiting limousine, compliments of Max's publisher.

You could say he was taking charge. And she let him. Her weeping had wiped out all her fighting power. What an embarrassing, disgraceful scene! Her emotions weren't for public consumption and she'd made a spectacle of herself. She sighed, but couldn't think of a thing to do about it now save forget it. She closed her eyes and leaned back against the soft cushions. She heard Max give the chauffeur Mary Lou's address, then the sounds of glasses and bottles and the pouring of drinks.

'Here, drink this,' he said, and she opened her eyes and took the glass from him. Vodka on ice. It was what she had been drinking at the party yesterday.

'Thanks.'

Well, let him take care of her. What was wrong with that? And surely Max was an expert in taking care of women. She didn't feel very strong and liberated right now and eating dinner out was a good idea. The bleak alternative was spending the evening alone at the Valentines' vast and gleaming penthouse apartment. Mary Lou and her husband Conrad were attending a business function and wouldn't be back until late.

At the apartment, Katrina went to her room to shower and change from her jeans and sweater into some more appropriate attire. While she primped, Max had a drink and watched the evening news on television.

She dressed in a jade-green mini, a soft knit affair of a sensuous blend of silk and cashmere that hugged her body closely. It was simple and understated, yet very much *there*. She'd gained several more pounds and she was beginning to lose that hungry look. She wore long, dangling earrings with a number of small diamonds that sparkled enthusiastically in the light, more diamonds at her throat, and high-heeled Italian shoes at her feet. Her short hair gleamed like black silk. Her dark eyes looked large and luminous with a sheen of sadness. She dabbed some Joy on various strategic places and she was ready to face the evening. She examined herself in the mirror one last time.

She was going out with the illustrious Max Killain, author of adventure novels. She made a face at herself. Just you don't forget he is the same man who almost bodily threw you out of his house when you wanted to give him back his papers, she told herself. And that every woman in sight wants him.

He's the wrong man for you. Just keep yourself coolly polite and a shade aloof. Don't let him dazzle you with his charm.

* * *

He dazzled her with his charm.

Alone at a secluded table there were no distractions. No other women fawning over him. No phone calls from distraught sisters. No computer calling him back to work. No Isabel. All there was was the two of them and it was magic.

They talked. She told him about her plans to start a nursery growing herbs on St Barlow and he told her how he had got started in photography—with a twenty-dollar camera given to him by his stepfather, the dairy farmer.

He took pictures of everything: clouds, dead skunks on the road, cows, tractors, his sisters when they weren't watching.

The food was delicious and she discovered she was hungry after all. He went on telling her about the film that was being made of his newly released book. The candles threw a warm golden light on his features and she loved watching him, loved listening to his voice.

It was a wonderful evening.

Afterwards, he took her up to the apartment, which was still empty. Mary Lou and Conrad had not yet come home.

'Would you like a drink before you go back?' she asked and he shook his head.

'No, I'd better go now.' He gave a half-smile. She wasn't sure what it meant.

'I enjoyed dinner,' she said. 'Thank you.'

'Come here,' he said huskily and drew her into his arms. He covered her mouth with his and pressed her body against him. She felt the tension in him, the passion in his kiss, and it was exhilarating and she couldn't feel her feet any more, as if she were floating somehow. She kissed him back and all she could think of was how wonderful it was to feel this wanted, and how very much she wanted him.

He released her suddenly. For a long moment he said nothing, his eyes dark.

'Tomorrow I'll come and help you with your things,' he said then. 'I'll bring us something to eat, all right?'

She swallowed. There was a message in his eyes, a message in his voice, and she was well aware of it. 'All right,' she heard herself say.

He smiled at her. 'Goodnight, Katrina.'

'Goodnight, Max.'

After he had left she stood still for a long moment, waiting for her heart to calm down, waiting for sanity to return.

Her sanity never quite returned. Granted, all the next day she wanted to call him and tell him not to come, that she had finished what needed to be done and she didn't need him, but she never quite managed to make the call. Everything was conspiring against her. She had very little time. She spent the morning with real-estate people, had lunch with a friend, had a facial and a hair-styling in the afternoon. She couldn't find a phone, or if she did it was being used, or out of order, or she had no coins. Wasn't that always the way it went? Never a phone when you really needed one. And that in New York City. Unbelievable.

So there she was, at almost six, back at the mansion, chatting with Mrs Pennybaker and having a late cup of tea, waiting, with her heart in her throat, for Max.

He arrived at six-thirty, carrying a box, which he took straight up to her room.

'We can eat while we work,' he said.

Nonsense, of course. He had a veritable feast of delicacies in the box, and wine, and glasses and a tablecloth and a bud vase with a single red rose and two tall white candles. All set up on a small table it was lovely and romantic and what you needed to do was sit down and enjoy it.

Which they did, but not right away, because it was still a little early for the civilised enjoyment of fancy food. They had a drink while they sorted stuffed toys into boxes. There was an endless supply of them—bears and monkeys and ducks and puppies and tigers in all sizes and shapes, even a koala bear given to her by an Australian friend of her father's. Enough to supply three or four orphanages, in fact. They taped and labelled boxes.

'I can take some of these back on the plane with me,' he said. 'Then you'll know they'll get there.'

Shipments of goods sometimes mysteriously disappeared and never made it to the addressee. Sometimes, magically, the vanished goods would reappear in the open markets or small shops of neighbouring islands. It was a puzzle, but one best avoided.

'When are you going back?' asked Katrina, wrapping a baby chimpanzee in pink tissue paper.

'Monday. I've got to get back to work; I'm behind schedule. Any idea when you'll be back?'

'I'm planning to leave next week Saturday.' She had to get back too. There were greenhouses to build and herbs to grow. She smiled at the thought. It was a lovely thought: she, Katrina, back in the warm sunlight, growing herbs for a living. It was a vision of gentleness and purity, living surrounded by lovely green plants, breathing air full of the fragrance of thyme and basil and lemon balm. 'I can't wait to get back,' she said. 'Imagine this—I'll be a contributing member of society, working for a living.'

He smiled at her. 'Does the idea appeal to you?'

'Actually, it does.' And what made her feel even better was that the business would create jobs for people. Not hundreds and thousands, of course, but some. She enjoyed the beauty and serenity of the island and now that she lived there it was good to be able to give something back.

He raised his glass. 'To your every success in the business world,' he said.

There was a tension in the air, a sense of expectation she'd felt ever since he had arrived. It wasn't strange, of course. She knew what was going to happen and she was allowing it to happen. She had not made the phone call.

They had dinner, but she was aware of being nervous. She had never been seduced before. It was quite an exhilarating thought: seduced!

And she was going to let it happen.

Men had tried, of course. Especially men who'd been aware of Bastian's long absences. 'Poor thing,' they'd said, 'you must be so lonely!' They'd assumed they were doing her a favour by offering their services for a night's pleasure. It wasn't the kind of pleasure she'd ever been interested in. She wanted the more permanent kind, backed up with love and trust. She was a romantic. A disillusioned romantic, yes, but still a romantic.

'Thank you for all this,' she said after they'd eaten, gesturing at the table, the food, the candles. 'Are you a closet romantic?'

'A closet romantic?' His mouth curved. 'That's not the way I'd describe it. Let's just say I have moments of great romantic inspiration.' He came to his feet, took her hand and pulled her from her chair straight into his arms. 'And you, Katrina, are a source of great inspiration.'

His mouth brushed over hers, sensuously, tantalisingly. His tongue touched the corners of her mouth, teasing.

She could not resist this man. She wanted him close, she wanted his strength and determination. She wanted to be part of him, to hold him to her always. To encircle him with her arms and never let him go.

Then he put his mouth against her cheek, close by her ear. 'Do you know how much I want to make love to you?' he asked softly.

'Yes,' she whispered. She felt herself begin to tremble.

'And what about you?' he went on, his tongue stroking her earlobe. 'Do you want to make love to me?'

'Yes,' she whispered. 'You know I do.' And he'd given her time to back out of it, time to prepare for it.

'So why are you so nervous?'

'I don't know,' she whispered.

His arms tightened around her. 'Don't worry about responsibility, Katrina. I'm a very responsible person.'

'I know,' she said. 'Thank you.' It sounded a little awkward, but the moment was gone, swallowed up in another kiss, less playful, more urgent.

She wanted to make love with Max more than anything else. But making love would make her vulnerable. She would be naked before him—not just her body, but her soul as well. She could not hold back part of herself, pretend it was merely a game that was over the moment the physical contact was broken.

She could not bear that, not ever again.

So much of herself had been locked away—love and trust and loyalty, gifts of the soul. Yet she didn't want them to be hidden forever. She could not live if she could never give them again to another man.

Max was kissing her, his hands sliding under her sweater—warm, strong hands. Could she trust him? What if she was making a mistake? What if this was just another sham? Her body tensed.

He must have felt it because he withdrew slightly and looked into her face, and his eyes darkened. 'What's wrong?' he asked softly.

She swallowed. 'I'm scared,' she whispered.

'Why?'

She closed her eyes. 'I'll be so...naked.'

There was a silence and she opened her eyes and looked at him, but he wasn't laughing. There was a look of great tenderness in his eyes, and he pulled her face against the warmth of his neck.

'I won't betray you,' he said softly, his voice a little husky. She sensed the sincerity of his words, knew deep in her heart that he spoke the truth. She might not know everything there was to know about this man, but she knew he was a man of integrity and loyalty. A quietness settled in her heart and she felt the fear flow away.

He was stroking her hair, very gently, and she relaxed against him, her body moulding itself against his. There was no yesterday, no tomorrow. There was only the present and she was feeling very, very good.

'You said you were very inspired,' she whispered.

'Yes,' he said against her cheek. She could feel him smile.

'Show me,' she whispered.

CHAPTER EIGHT

MAX took her clothes off slowly, his fingers caressing her bare skin as he exposed it. His own clothes followed hers, landing on top in an intimate tangle on a chair. They were standing together, naked, and Katrina shivered slightly. Not from cold, but from the sheer wonder of the moment.

He had said she was beautiful, the night he had looked at her for the first time on the island. Now she was seeing him too, and certainly he was also beautiful, his strong, muscled body standing there in the faint glow of the moon that slanted through the window. She stared at him, taking in the clean, sculpted lines of his body, like a Greek statue. He reached for her and his strong arms encircled her and pressed her close. It was a glorious feeling—the heat of his skin against hers, his mouth kissing hers. Her knees felt weak. Her head was dizzy. She couldn't stand any longer.

He laid her on the bed, lying on his side next to her, looking down at her. 'Just let me look at you and touch you,' he said and he took her fingers and kissed each one, then the inside of her wrist. He began to touch her, slow, sensual hands stroking with feathery caresses—her cheek, her throat, her breast, her stomach. She closed her eyes and let the feeling take over—a delicious sensation tingling through her body.

She could not lie still for long. She stirred restlessly. She needed to touch him, feel and taste him with her own hands and mouth. 'I want to touch you too,' she whispered, turning towards him, reaching out to touch his mouth, tracing the shape of it with her index finger, then moving down and spreading her hand on his brown chest, feeling the crinkly hair curling against her fingers. She searched for his mouth and kissed him, showing him her response, her hunger, and she felt a shudder go through him.

They clung together, kissing feverishly, their hands exploring each other restlessly. Ah, the wonder of touch, the wonder of feeling! She felt alive and aglow, her every nerve-end vibrant with sensation. Her body moved, responding to the magic of some primitive music inside her.

Then she felt his lips on her breast. His mouth was hot on her nipples, his tongue setting off sparks of fire. 'Ah,' she breathed, and a low moan came from deep inside him in answer, and all sense of time was lost.

Such ecstasy, such exquisite delight! The magic of it all delighted her. Something broke free inside her. She let herself fly and the freedom was so wonderful, the feeling that she was giving herself freely, with passion and need and trust. The feeling that she truly wanted this man who took so much time, so much loving care with her body, who seemed to delight in the senses the way she did—touch and smell and taste.

She had never felt the deep caring and honest loving she was feeling now. She felt treasured in his arms, treasured and completely entranced. And she wanted to give herself, offer herself, wanted him close, wanted him inside her, to hold him in the most intimate way of loving.

His breathing was slow and ragged, his movements more urgent, less controlled. Arms and legs entangled, their bodies damp, they pleasured each other with increasing fervour. The tension mounted with every kiss and touch, a desperate yearning claiming them both. Her body pulsed and throbbed. She tangled her hands in the thickness of his hair, arching herself against him, feeling passion evaporate the last shreds of reasoned thought, obliterating all sense of time and place. She let it happen.

'Please,' she murmured. He moved over her and they melded together in primal ritual, finding ancient rhythms that swept them up into a wave of passion—higher and higher until it crested like a great ocean wave, exploding into a thousand sparks glittering in the sunlight.

Then there was silence and they lay in each other's arms, exhausted and sated, but not ready to let go. Her cheek nestled against his chest, she could hear the steady beating of his heart.

Magic, she thought drowsily. We make magic together.

She awoke in the middle of the night, not knowing what had drawn her from sleep. Maybe it was the subconscious sensation of someone else in her bed. She came fully awake, savouring the awareness of Max's presence beside her, the warmth of his body against hers. She smiled into the darkness, her heart flowing over with a rich, sweet emotion.

A strange lightness seemed to come from outside. She carefully slipped out of bed and peeked through the curtains, smiling with the sudden wonder of the view. Snow had fallen during the night—two inches, no more, but everything was washed in white, a layer of pristine purity that transformed the gardens outside and the buildings beyond in a fairy-tale wonderland. Every branch and twig was covered and the full moon silvered the trees. Everything was perfectly still. Not a breeze stirred the trees, not a sound came from anywhere. It was magical.

It's an omen. The thought came to her out of nowhere and made her smile. The past had been washed clean and she had been given a new beginning.

She slipped back into bed and Max reached out in sleep, drawing her into his arms, against the warmth of his body.

It was the perfect place to be.

In the morning they made love again, the desire springing up as soon as they awoke and became aware of each other. Afterwards they went downstairs into the kitchen, made coffee and went back into bed to nurse the brew in leisurely relaxation.

They were out of the house before the Pennybakers arrived in the kitchen and they spent all day together in the city, walking 57th Street and browsing through the bookshops and art galleries, passing up on the antique shops. She was sick of looking at antiques, she said. Max was attentive and funny and made her laugh. It felt good to laugh. It felt good to have all this attention showered upon her.

They lunched at the Russian Tea Room, sitting in a red velvet booth, trying to warm their frozen hands and toes. Over a bowl of hot borscht, he asked her to come to Vermont with him the next day and spend the weekend with his family. She said yes. Imagine meeting the Parasite Sisters! She was dying with curiosity!

Despite the cold, it was a wonderful day. Now that Max wasn't actually writing his book, he was relaxed and at ease. It was suddenly difficult to remember how insufferable he had been on the island and how very much she hadn't wanted him around. Well, that was what she'd tried to tell herself.

They had pre-dinner drinks in a cosy little jazz bar in the Village and listened to the musicians improvising. They didn't know anyone in the place and the anonymity was bliss. Max was holding her hand on the table. It made her smile. This was like a real romance. No, it *was* a real romance—walking together holding hands, smiling into each other's eyes, telling stories, making each other laugh, stealing kisses at street corners, waiting for the lights to change. She couldn't remember ever having spent a day like this alone with Bastian—just enjoying each other's company, exploring shops and galleries, having a leisurely lunch with just the two of them. Not even during their honeymoon.

Somehow, there had always been other people, old friends to visit, new ones made. Bastian had been gregarious and lively. He was always asking people to join them for dinner, for a drink. Bastian had never been comfortable being alone. Not even with her.

She put her glass down and Max squeezed her hand. The sharp angles of his face had softened in the warm light of the candle. 'You look sad,' he said. 'Did I say something?'

She shook her head. 'I was thinking how much I'm enjoying this day with just the two of us.'

'And that makes you sad?'

'No.' She bit her lip, hesitating. She could not mention Bastian now. It was against all the rules of proper etiquette to bring up old lovers while having a good time with a new one. Besides that, it was in bad taste.

'Tell me,' he urged.

'I was thinking that in six years of marriage I never spent a day like this with Bastian. Not even on our honeymoon.' There, she had said it, bad taste or not. She looked down on his hand covering hers. 'Sorry.'

'Don't be.'

And then she found herself talking about Bastian. She hadn't wanted to, really. It didn't seem right. Only it did.

She told him how her young girl's dreams had been evaporated in the harsh light of reality.

'He was always taking off on long trips, leaving me at home. It wasn't the kind of marriage I'd had in mind. Now and then he'd grace the apartment with his presence.' She looked down into her glass. 'I didn't feel like a wife. I felt like a mistress, a kept woman, someone conveniently tucked away for whenever he might need me. It wasn't good for my ego, believe me.'

'I believe you,' said Max. He ordered another whisky. Maybe he needed the fortification.

'It didn't take me long to figure out what was going on,' she went on, knowing there was no stopping now. 'Then I started trying to find ways to make the marriage work, which was pretty naïve. It was a lost cause, of course.'

'What kind of marriage did you have in mind?'

'The kind where, for starters, you're faithful to each other. You go to bed together at night and wake up together in the morning on a more regular basis. Once every couple of months doesn't do it.'

His face was expressionless. 'Did you discuss this with him?' His voice seemed calm and emotionless.

'Oh, sure, but he wasn't interested. He was happy the way things were. He pointed out that there was nothing wrong with him, or the marriage. There was something wrong with my expectations. They were much too bourgeois, too limiting, too soul-destroying. You get the idea.'

'I get the idea.'

'He refused to acknowledge problems. He just laughed at everything. I couldn't even have a good all-out marital fight with him and clear the air. All I could do was kick the Italian furniture and cry in the shower.'

Oh, how she had cried! Until she'd come to her senses and decided that Bastian wasn't worth the expenditure of all those tears. He wasn't worth her spending so much energy on trying to make things work. There was nothing to make work. She'd packed up her emotions—her love, trust, loyalty—in a secret corner of her heart, thinking that maybe one day there would be someone worthy to give them to.

Max was listening with a dark frown. 'How long were you going to put up with that?'

'Not much longer. I was trying to find a way to divorce him *in absentia*.' She smiled brightly. 'Enough. Let's change the subject.'

So they changed the subject, finished their drink, and went in search of a restaurant for dinner, finding an obscure little place that looked like something out of the Arabian Nights with lots of brass and Persian rugs on the walls. They ate lamb kebabs and rice with pine nuts and other Middle Eastern delicacies while they listened to the monotonous yet seductive wail of Arabian music in the background.

'Where to now?' he asked when they'd finished their meal. He led her outside into the frigid winter night. 'A movie? A nightclub? You want to go dancing?'

'After an hour in this place? My senses are overdosed.' She shivered in the cold and hugged her coat around her.

'All right,' he said, 'then I know just the right place. It's warm, quiet and private.'

He took her to his hotel, to a sumptuous suite, where a large bouquet of red roses stood on the coffee-table.

He took her in his arms. 'The roses are for you,' he said in her ear. 'Stay with me tonight. The whole night.'

'I'd like that,' she said. It was the truth.

She showered off the New York City dirt in a rose marble bathroom stocked with Guerlain toiletries and piles of huge, fluffy rose-coloured towels. When she came out of the bathroom, wrapped in one of the soft white bathrobes furnished by the hotel, she found that Max had ordered a bottle of Dom Pérignon and found some romantic music on the radio.

She was being wooed. The thought made her smile. She sat back on the sofa and closed her eyes, letting the music flow through her while she waited for him to come out of the bathroom.

It was all too good to be true, of course. Happiness of this sort never lasted, did it?

Well, how would she know? It had never happened before. Not quite like this.

Not quite like this, she thought later as she lay on the enormous bed, light-headed with champagne and love, savouring his hands on her body, his mouth on hers. Not ever like this.

She spent an insightful, intriguing weekend at the farm, a slightly ramshackle house full of women who descended on Max like an avalanche the moment he stepped out of the limo.

They talked incessantly, while he sat and listened, or pretended to, doled out advice, encouraged, interceded, made phone calls, handed out cheques. They all had *very* important matters to discuss with him, including his slightly dizzy mother and his ancient grandmother, and they were constantly competing for his time and attention. His twin sisters were in college, but both had come home for the weekend, knowing Big Brother, as they called him, was home to visit.

It was a warm and lively household, not too neat and tidy, and definitely not very well organised. The cooking, what there was of it, left a lot to be desired. But everyone was happy and cheerful and they loved music. They played the piano and the guitar and sang songs and laughed a lot. They took Katrina in as a matter of course. What was, after all, one more woman?

That night she shared a large attic room with the twins, who told her all their love troubles as if she were a long-lost friend who needed to be brought up to date, and they sat up till two in the morning, drinking cheap white wine and eating crisps, making crumbs all over the beds.

It was not the sort of female bonding Katrina was familiar with. It was wonderful. Katrina actually found herself liking his sisters. It was amazing. She had been fully prepared to detest the Parasite Sisters, as she had secretly named them, but there it was. They were funny and wacky and they loved their brother, in their own unique way.

His grandmother was a tiny old woman with the gift of gab and many words of wisdom in search of receptive ears, which were not always available. She loved quoting Shakespeare and Socrates, and on occasion the Beatles. The very important matter she wanted to discuss with Max was the fact that her patience was running out.

'Patience with what?' asked Max.

'With you,' she said. 'I want you to get married before I die.'

'Then I have plenty of time,' said Max. 'You're only ninety-two.'

Her wrinkled finger pointed at Katrina. 'What about her? She looks all right to me. A little skinny, maybe.'

'She won't have me,' said Max.

His grandmother peered at Katrina with sharp black eyes. 'Why not?'

'He's much too perfect for me,' said Katrina in a brilliant flash of inspiration. She smiled sweetly.

His grandmother chuckled. 'You've never lived with him, have you, dear?'

One lie begot another. 'No,' said Katrina bravely.

'Try it, then, and you'll see he's not perfect. Then you can marry him. I don't suppose you're perfect yourself? Perfect people are so boring.'

'She's not boring,' said Max. 'Believe me.'

'Excellent,' said his grandmother. 'I'll be happy to take you into the family, girl.'

'Thank you,' said Katrina. It was nice to be accepted, and what else could she say?

The old lady's eyes gleamed with humour. 'We all live a bit on the fringe, as you may have noticed.'

'I have,' said Katrina.

On Sunday night, late, they arrived back at his hotel where they spent another glorious night together. On Monday morning he dropped her off at Mary Lou's and went straight to the airport to start his trip back to St Barlow.

She felt bereft, miserable, lonely. She took a taxi back to the mansion. The house had never seemed more cold and sad despite all the gleam and glitter of wealth. She couldn't wait to get back to St Barlow. But it would take at least several more days before everything was finalised. But Saturday, come hell or high water, she was getting on a plane.

Monday passed painfully slowly. Tuesday dragged. Wednesday didn't want to come to an end. At five o'clock, as she was buying a magazine at a news-stand, it seemed to stop altogether. Not only did time stop, her heart seemed to stop as well.

Frozen to the pavement, she stared at the tabloid newspaper on the rack in front of her. Two faces, close together, smiled back at her from the cover photo. One was Max's, the other Cassandra's.

The headline took up almost half the page. BACK TOGETHER AGAIN! it screamed.

CHAPTER NINE

SOMEBODY shoved a briefcase into Katrina's ribs, waking her up out of her stupor. No apology was offered and the man grabbed a newspaper, slapped some money down and was gone again. Such friendly people, the New Yorkers. Probably a stockbroker down on his luck, she thought, rubbing her ribs. There were a lot of those these days.

She glanced again at the tabloid. The picture was still there, and the faces belonged to Max and Cassandra. Not a figment of her imagination, as she had hoped for one wild moment.

However, maybe the article was a figment of the imagination of the paper. A tabloid was after all only a tabloid and tabloids were not to be believed. Everybody knew that. Some of them made up their own sleazy photographs by pasting the face of one person on to the body of someone else. They printed pieces of dialogue out of context so they ended up implying things that had never been said or intended. Sometimes they created witnesses by paying people to lie. Money could work magic.

She, Katrina, widow of the infamous Bastian MacKenzie, playboy of international notoriety, knew all about it.

So why didn't she simply shrug her shoulders and walk away? Why, horrors of horrors, did she fish some money out of her coat pocket and for the very first time ever in her life actually *buy* one of the offending rags?

* * *

160

Cassandra Marble and Max Killain had attended a party at the luxurious Fifth Avenue apartment of Mr and Mrs Conrad Valentine, the article said. They had been spotted dining at an out-of-the-way Italian restaurant and holding hands. There was a witness who had seen them in a Toronto hotel together.

Katrina was sitting in Mary Lou's exquisite sitting-room, with the paper spread out on the large marble coffee-table, trying to get a grip on herself. Mary Lou was getting her a drink to help her towards that goal.

'It's all lies,' said Mary Lou, handing her a glass of vodka and tonic. 'You know that.'

'Of course I know that. So why do I feel as if I want to strangle him?'

'Because you think there is a possibility that there's some truth to it.'

'Do you?'

Mary Lou shrugged. 'Who knows?'

'You're a lot of help.'

'Hey, I try.' She took the bottle and poured herself a drink too.

Conrad came home, took one look at the tabloid picture, at the weeping Katrina and the drink-pouring Mary Lou and fled into his study.

Later that night, Katrina lay in bed, plotting. She was going to go to the island and throw Max out of the house after she had destroyed his files on the computer. She'd had enough. Bastian had done this to her, and she wasn't taking it from any other man. No more tabloid pictures, no more women, no more *nothing*!

She wept into her pillow until, exhausted, she fell asleep. The next morning, after two cups of strong Jamaican coffee, she felt more reasonable. When you weighed not much more than a hundred pounds, you didn't throw out two hundred pounds of male. First, you'd try talking to him.

After all, shouldn't she ask for an explanation? Should she not give him the benefit of the doubt?

No, no way, never again. That was what she had done with Bastian and she'd wanted to believe him. It had been pathetic. She was not going to go through that humiliating process again. She might no longer have an ancestral home, a lot of money and precious antiques, but she did have her pride.

She'd get a plane out on Friday, a day early, but she could manage. She had all day to finish up details and pack. She couldn't stand being here for a day longer.

As she sat on the plane, forcing down food and drink, her moods swung back and forth between hope and despair. It was all just a pack of lies. She'd find him in his office, typing away. Then he would see her and leap out of his chair and kiss her senseless, take her to his room and make passionate love to her. He only wanted her.

She could almost believe it.

But not quite.

She felt sick. Her stomach hurt, her head ached. Not even the glorious emerald and turquoise waters below could calm her.

She was going insane.

She needed help.

'Is there anything I can get you?' the flight attendant asked, smiling.

'I'd like a cup of sage tea. Red sage, if you have it.'

The woman's eyes widened. 'I'm sorry, we don't have that. Can I bring you some regular tea?'

She shook her head. 'It won't do me any good. It's got to be sage. It cures insanity.'

'Insanity?' The woman began to look a little worried.
'Yes, and it's good for ulcers and night sweats too.'

The attendant fled and Katrina looked out of the
window and grinned, feeling better for the moment.

In Barbados, Fish was waiting for her. Fish was a huge
black American from Chicago who had started his own
puddle-jumper service with a friend from Trinidad. In
their twin-engine planes they could reach tiny islands with
landing strips not adequate for larger planes. Fish had
a shaved head, a broad smile, laughing eyes and tall tales
to tell. Flying with him was never boring, and now more
than ever she was happy to be diverted by his stories.

She arrived on St Barlow late that afternoon and, despite her nerves being frazzled and frayed, it felt good
to be back. Home. It felt like coming home.

Mum's taxi, the only one on the island, was waiting,
and the driver sang reggae songs all the way to the house,
which kept the conversation to a minimum. The driver
helped her take out the boxes and bags full of toys, took
her payment and was off with a wave and a grin. Katrina
found her key and opened the front door. She left the
boxes where they were and moved inside the house, her
heart suddenly racing with fearful anticipation.

She heard music, and she stopped for a moment and
listened. It wasn't Mrs Blackett singing hymns, and it
wasn't any kind of music that Max listened to.

Then she saw. A portable tape deck on the small table
on the veranda. And on the lounger next to it a woman
in a black bikini.

It wasn't hard to guess who. She couldn't see the face,
but she could see the big, curly mop of black hair.

Cassandra Marble.

CHAPTER TEN

FOR a moment Katrina couldn't breathe. Her heart gave a frightening lurch, then seemed to stop altogether. It was as if all the life had been sucked out of her. Then she gulped in air like a drowning victim and her whole body began to shake. She trembled so badly that she had to lean on to the hall table in order not to sag on to the floor tiles like a swooning eighteenth-century damsel in distress.

Fortunately, her mind was firmly anchored in the twentieth century and it took control after a short lapse of weakness. Get a grip on yourself, baby, it said. You've gone through this before, you can do it again.

She took a couple of steadying breaths and got a grip on herself. She tested her legs and then slowly, carefully moved up the stairs to her room. No sounds came from Max's study as she passed his door. Where was he? Sitting on the side of her bed, she calmed herself some more. In fact she was so calm that it was scary. She felt cold. Her heart felt like a chunk of ice lodged in her chest. Her mind was crystal-clear like the frigid waters of a mountain stream.

She came to her feet again and checked out the various rooms. Max was not to be found in either his study or his bedroom. She moved on to the next room and found what she had searched for: Cassandra's stuff. Her clothes hung neatly in the cupboard. A purple and black flowered négligé lay draped over a chair. Bottles and jars of cosmetics had been set out on the dressing-table.

Cassandra had taken possession of the room as if she had every right to be there. Katrina felt herself freeze some more. The woman had invaded her territory, her home, her haven of tranquillity. It was not to be tolerated.

She took a deep breath. She needed a plan. She needed, above all, to keep her dignity. It was the only way to deal with the situation. Dignity had saved her through her years with Bastian. Somehow, she had managed to hang on to her self-respect.

She knew just what to do.

Quickly she threw off her city clothes and pulled on a light cotton dress—a shower would have to wait. She fixed her make-up and ran a comb through her hair and she was ready for battle.

She straightened her spine and went back downstairs. Head high, she walked confidently across the sitting-room and out on to the veranda and produced a charming smile.

'Cassandra!' she said. 'What a surprise!'

Cassandra jerked up from her slumber. For a moment her eyes widened in shock as she looked up at Katrina standing over her.

'Katrina!' she said then, her control back. 'How nice to see you!'

Katrina sat down and leaned casually back in her chair, all calm and relaxed. Well, that was what she was pretending. 'Where's Max?' she asked. 'Swimming?'

'He went to Barbados. He'll be back this afternoon some time. Oh, I do hope I'm not inconveniencing you dropping in like this; it's just that...' Cassandra let her voice face away.

'Not in the least,' said Katrina nicely. 'It's a quiet island. I like having guests. So tell me, what brings you here?'

'I needed a break.' Cassandra looked pained. 'My writing isn't going well, and I couldn't think of a place to go. My villa in the south of France is being done by JPP right now, and I can't bear New York at this time of the year. I can't stand the cold. Anyway, when I heard about Max escaping to St Barlow, I thought it seemed the perfect place to go.'

With Max being here, of course it was.

'It's lovely here,' agreed Katrina, surveying the view of crystalline waters and the white crescent beach below with its palms lazily wafting in the breeze. She took in a deep breath. The air was clean and smelled of flowers.

Cassandra shifted into a more upright position and tossed her long dark hair over her shoulders. 'I'm considering buying a house here myself. I just know I'll be able to work better here.'

Oh, God, what a nightmare of an idea. Katrina felt her body tense.

'It's perfect,' she said. 'It's so quiet. No casinos or clubs or restaurants, no nightlife at all. Absolutely nothing going on to distract you.' She smiled reassuringly. 'We do have a small teaching hospital, though. Very up-to-date. They're especially fond of exotic tropical ailments—parasites, amoebas, fungi—so if you catch any of these you're in the right place.'

For a fraction of a moment Cassandra looked uncertain, or maybe she'd imagined it.

Katrina leaned forward in her chair, looking earnest. 'Would you like me to help you find a place? I know who to talk to.' She also knew there wasn't a single villa for sale, nor would there be for a while to come.

Surprise flickered in Cassandra's eyes. 'Would you really?'

'Of course I would!' Katrina said, her voice full of goodwill and charity. 'It will be fun having you here.

Someone to talk to. It does get lonely at times.' She came to her feet. 'I'm going to see if I can find myself a rum punch; how about you?'

'A rum punch would be lovely,' said Cassandra, and Katrina left the veranda. Her knees were shaking with nerves. Putting on a show like this could take the strength out of you. However, she'd gone through worse.

She went to the kitchen where she found Mrs Blackett getting ready to prepare dinner. She was happy to see Katrina, and said she hoped it was all right that she had prepared a room for her friend Cassandra. Of course, said Katrina.

She took a pitcher of rum punch, already mixed up, and some glasses and took them back to the veranda. She heard a car come up the drive as she was pouring the drinks and the next moment Max came leaping up the wooden stairs, carrying a small overnight bag. He stopped dead in his tracks when he saw the two of them. His eyes narrowed.

'Well,' he said then, 'this is a surprise.'

Katrina could imagine. She gave him a bright smile. 'Hi,' she said cheerily. Her heart was breaking. This was not the reunion she had envisaged, with one of his other women present. He looked so good, so vital, with his hair falling over his forehead and his blue eyes bright as the sky.

'I thought you'd be back tomorrow,' he said, his face tense.

'Ah, "the best laid schemes o' mice an' men",' she said lightly. 'Would you care for a rum punch?'

'No, thank you,' he said coolly. 'If you two will excuse me, I have work to do.' He disappeared into the house.

Katrina sighed elaborately. 'I can feel another attack coming on.'

'Attack?' Cassandra frowned. 'What kind of attack?'

'The kind Max goes through when he's writing. He becomes absolutely possessed and the best thing to do is to stay out of his way. He sort of loses touch with reality and becomes impossible to live with. Haven't you ever noticed?'

Cassandra smiled. 'I like my men a bit wild. What real woman doesn't?'

'True,' agreed Katrina. I've got to get away from that witch, she thought, or I'll pour my drink over her permed head. She pushed her chair back. 'I'd better check with Mrs Blackett about dinner.'

Mrs Blackett didn't need checking, so she went to her room instead. She passed Max's office and heard him moving around. She went into her room and sat on the edge of the bed. Her eyes caught the tabloid paper sticking out of her holdall. Mrs Blackett must have taken her things upstairs. She pulled the paper out and looked at it once more, then flung it on the floor.

'Damn you, Max,' she muttered, and the door flew open and there he was, looming in front of her as if she had summoned him rather than cursed him.

'What the hell is going on here?' he demanded, his voice barely controlled. His face was furious, his eyes shooting blue sparks of anger at her. A man thwarted. It was quite a sight.

'I'd like to know that too,' she said coolly. In the face of so much heat, she'd better produce a little cold.

He jammed his hands in his pockets. 'What the hell is that woman doing here? Are you out of your mind inviting her here to stay? Don't I have trouble enough when I go home? I come here to work! To have some peace and quiet and get away from all these damned females!'

Oh, God. She took a steadying breath. She needed to think. Was this a trick? Some brilliant scheme to throw her off?

'Answer me! What the hell is she doing here?'

She looked straight into his eyes. 'She's looking for a villa. She wants to stay on the island. She thinks she'll be able to work better here.'

His eyes shot fire. 'And so you *invited* her here? Are you crazy?'

She was getting quite enough of his rudeness. 'I didn't invite her! When I came home this afternoon, there she was, sitting on the veranda in her skimpy bikini waiting for you to come home from Barbados. Naturally, I thought *you* had invited her here.'

He looked at her as if he thought she'd lost her mind. 'You think *I* invited her? Why would I do something so insane?'

'Perhaps for the simple reason you wanted her here.' She picked the paper up from the floor and thrust it at him. 'Look at this.'

He glanced at the paper. 'This is absurd! For God's sake, Katrina, you don't *read* this trash, do you?'

'That *is* a picture of you, is it?'

'Yes.'

'And that is your body under that face, is it?'

'*What*?'

'Just checking if your head is sitting on the right body. They play tricks like that sometimes.'

He glanced down at the photo again. 'It's me. And Cassandra is Cassandra. That picture was taken years ago at a publisher's party.' He glanced up again. 'What is all this? What's going on?'

'If you didn't invite her then it must be because she is in pursuit of you. She did seem quite interested in you at the Valentines' party.'

He groaned. 'That's all I need. How did she know how to find me? I sure as hell didn't tell anyone I'm hiding out here.'

Katrina shrugged. 'Maybe Mary Lou mentioned it.'

He flung the paper on the floor with disgust. 'She's got to go,' he said with cold determination. 'I've had it up to here with women.' He turned on his heel and marched to the door.

'Max!' she called. 'What are you going to do?'

He glanced at her over his shoulder. 'I'm going to throw her off the island is what I'm going to do.'

An hour later the two of them sat down at the table to eat the dinner cooked for three. Fried flying fish, rice and breadfruit fritters. Max had disposed of Cassandra in record time, but it had done nothing for his mood. He seemed distracted and morose.

'What did you do with her?' Katrina asked, taking a bite of rice.

'I took her to the landing strip. Fish was still there. I made it worth his while to haul her off any place he wanted to go and to put her on his blacklist.'

That should keep her away for good, Katrina thought. She ate her fish and thought about the picture in the tabloid.

'I wonder where they got the idea of that article, and that picture?'

He gave her an impatient look. 'For heaven's sake, Katrina! Cassandra orchestrated it, of course. That woman is a menace.'

They finished their meal in silence. Not a cheerful silence to be sure. The air seemed filled with negative energy, not an atmosphere that bred love and charity. After dinner they went their separate ways, Max back to his study, and Katrina to the veranda with a stack of reading material about the cultivation of hydroponic herbs.

After all, if you weren't making passionate love with the man of your dreams, you had to find other things to fill the time.

Oh, damn, damn, she thought. The words on the page in front of her blurred. I can't take this. Not again.

The romantic interlude in New York might as well not have happened. The magic had gone. It seemed as if the very atmosphere in the house had been poisoned, as if an evil spell had been cast. All she could think of was to get away from the place.

She scarcely saw Max all weekend. He spent his time in his study in the throes of finishing his book, and she tramped around the island checking out available land and trying not to think about him.

The more she tried not to, the more she did. He was on her mind all the time. Like an obsession.

Oh, God, she thought, not an obsession. Obsessions were so difficult to get rid of. Hours and hours of psychotherapy. And there was no therapist on the island. The closest you'd get was Josephine, the conch-fritter vendor, who had quite a reputation of counselling neurotic clients, friends and family members.

By Monday Katrina was a nervous wreck, in spite of all the camomile tea she had consumed, in spite of all the long hours of trying to be rational. Max was not the man for her. He was too popular with the women. A relationship with him would only cause her recurring heartache. She should simply stop loving him. She took inventory of his vices: he was impatient, overbearing, a workaholic, et cetera, et cetera.

Nothing helped. All she could really think about was how much she wanted him. How much she wanted to make love. How much she wanted to feel his mouth make magic with hers. How much she wanted to spend the rest of her life with him. It was total madness.

Falling out of love was the only way to go. She'd thought about it reasonably and logically and she'd made up her mind. For the next two days, she managed quite successfully to avoid Max. It was not difficult to stay busy; there was so much to do and organise. At night she had dinner with Sasha and her husband, and afterwards they plotted and planned endlessly. Sasha was smart and funny and enthusiastic and they got along famously. She was lucky, so very lucky, to have Sasha on her side. She was going to make this business work—for herself, for other people. She was going to make something of herself. The seeds of ambition and idealism had sprouted inside her mind, shooting up to the sun, delicate, yet confident.

One morning Max caught her having breakfast.

'Good morning,' he said. He pulled up a chair and poured himself a cup of coffee. She watched his hand, her pulse leaping, her body tense.

'Good morning.' Birds twittered outside. Through the kitchen door, she heard Mrs Blackett singing about the joys of a new morning.

Max took a swallow of coffee. 'Katrina?'

She looked up, meeting his eyes. 'Yes?'

'You've been avoiding me,' he said.

She buttered a piece of toast. 'I've been very busy.' It was the truth.

'What we shared in New York was special,' he said slowly. 'I was looking forward to your coming back to the island. I'm sorry Cassandra had to spoil it.'

She did not reply. She didn't want to think about New York, about making love, about laughing together, about the glorious feeling of wonder. She wanted to be cool and calm, but she had the awful feeling she was going to lose it.

He put his cup down. 'So what has been wrong these last few days, Katrina?'

She bit her lip and took a deep breath. 'It's only become clear to me again that...that I was right all along. I think it's a mistake for me to be involved with you.' It sounded so calm, so reasonable.

'Why?'

Her hand began to tremble. She put her fork down. 'Because of who you are. And what you are. Bastian was surrounded by women all the time. I'm not going to deal with that again.' She swallowed painfully. 'Never!' There was a welling-up of emotion—a terrible mixture of anger and pain and fear. She wanted to break into tears and weep into her scrambled eggs. She wanted to scream at him. And that at seven in the morning. It was a disgrace. She swallowed back her tears and started shovelling in her eggs.

He scraped back his chair and stood up, jamming his hands in his pockets. 'For God's sake, Katrina! I am *not* Bastian! Why do you think I came to the island? Because I love to be surrounded by neurotic females? Because I *need* them?'

'No, I suppose you don't need them,' she said dully. 'And you don't need me either. You've got your precious Isabel.'

There was a loaded silence. Then he cursed under his breath and walked off into the kitchen, slamming the door so hard that it reverberated through the whole house.

Mrs Blackett stopped singing in the middle of her hymn. The morning had stopped being joyous.

*   *   *

Blood. Big, dark drops, on the tile floor of the sitting-room. Katrina stared down at them with a jolt of alarm. She'd just come out of the kitchen, where she'd discussed the secrets of bush medicine with Mrs Blackett while drinking a peaceful cup of afternoon tea. Seeing blood was not a peaceful sight.

Outside thunder rumbled through a darkening sky, an ominous omen. She shivered as she looked at the blood.

Somebody was bleeding. Max? Well, who else? Good God, what had happened? It was not a thought she wanted to dwell on. Hailing from New York City, images of carnage came to mind instinctively. Had somebody shot him? Had he shot himself? Maybe she would find a note...

'Stop it!' she said out loud to herself. She took a fortifying breath and glanced around. Max wasn't in the sitting-room, but it wouldn't be hard to find him—all she had to do was follow the trail of blood.

Across the living-room, up the stairs, into his bedroom. The door was open and there he was, sitting on the side of the bed in his wet swimming-shorts, holding a blood-soaked bandage against the big toe of his left foot.

'Quite a bloodbath,' she said, leaning against the doorpost in relief. It did not look fatal.

'It looks worse than it is,' he said, not looking at her.

'Can I help you?' So calm, so polite. Outside more thunder rumbled through the sky. It was going to be some rainstorm.

'I need another bandage. It's still bleeding.'

'What did you do?' She moved across the room into the adjoining bathroom and switched on the light. It was only just after four and the sudden darkness outside was eerie.

'I stepped on something in the water,' she heard him say. 'I was going for a swim. I don't know what it was, but it was sharp.'

There was blood all over the white floor and bath-tub. A pretty gruesome sight. She checked the medicine cabinet but there wasn't much of any use in there. She went back into the room.

'I'll get the first-aid kit. It's downstairs. I'll be right back.'

She found bandages, but the tube of ointment had been squeezed empty, and it was ancient. She rushed out of the door to the garden and pulled off a handful of echinacea leaves, then raced back up the stairs to Max's room.

She knelt in front of him, putting a towel under his foot. 'Let me do this. It's easier for me.' She was trying to be matter-of-fact. She didn't feel matter-of-fact. For the rest of her life, she was sure, she would never be able to be in control of her heart when she was close to this man, whether it was his mouth or his bleeding toe.

'What the hell have you got there?' he asked as she put the leaves down on a clean towel.

'Medicinal leaves. They're good for preventing infection.'

He groaned. 'What kind of leaves?'

'Echinacea. Coneflower, it's called, or rudbekia or Missouri snakeroot. The Indians used it for snakebite. You can make a tincture from the dried roots. That works even better. I'll just wrap it up with the leaves now and I'll fix up a hot poultice later.'

'Wouldn't a simple anti-bacterial ointment be easier?'

'If I had one, yes. But this is natural and just as good.'

She took off the blood-soaked bandage and examined the wound. A large cut, but not too deep. It looked clean.

'I let it bleed under the water to clean it out, and there's nothing in it,' he said. 'It's nothing to worry about.'

It probably wasn't. It looked as if it had stopped bleeding. She wet a piece of gauze and cleaned up around the cut, then covered it with a few leaves and bandaged it up.

'You're a witch doctor,' he said. 'Did you learn all that from your grandmother?'

'And from my mother. She grew all kinds of herbs and plants in our yard. Drove the gardeners crazy. It never fitted in with their landscaping designs and schemes. But then my mother wasn't one for fitting into any scheme herself.'

'Neither are you,' he said quietly.

He had a big, well-shaped foot, and it was cool to the touch. It was strange to sit here and touch him like this.

'Your hands feel warm,' he said, his voice very low.

She kept her eyes on what she was doing, not replying. Her heart was doing crazy things. Ah, the power of words, the power of touch!

'Feels good,' he went on.

She put on the last piece of tape. 'Done,' she said in as businesslike a voice as she could muster. 'Does it hurt?'

'Not bad.' He leaned forward and took her hands, lifting her off her knees. He let himself fall backwards on the bed and she landed neatly on top of him, her mouth against the warm skin of his bare chest. His arms encircled her, drew her higher up and then he was kissing her.

Not a tender, playful kiss, but one so full of desperate passion that it instantly devastated all her defences. Her body flooded with warm desire.

'I want you,' he murmured against her mouth. 'Oh, God, Katrina, I want you.'

He turned her over and then she lay beneath him and her common sense blew straight out of the window. He drew from her all her own buried need. All the yearning and hunger erupted from her soul and she clung to him, kissing him in wild abandon, aching with need for him.

He took off her shorts and shirt in a frantic series of moves, sliding, pulling, pushing, his mouth never leaving her body, kissing her mouth, her throat, her breasts, his mouth as urgent as his hands. His damp swimming-shorts came off and they lay together, their naked bodies feverish with need. They kissed and touched and stroked wordlessly, breathlessly, a primal force taking over, consuming them.

She clung to him blindly, trembling against the strength of his steel-hard body. All was sensation—fire and fever, a fierceness beyond all control.

The tension shattered as the rain broke loose from the sky, lashing down outside on the trees and greenery, saturating the hot, thirsty earth.

She lay breathless in his arms, unable to move, her limbs heavy, her body sated. If she'd ever wondered what it would feel like to be passionately ravished, she need wonder no longer. It felt wonderful.

They lay silent for a long time. His arms slipped away from her and she watched him as he turned on his back, eyes closed, exhausted. His hand searched for her, landing on her upper thigh, resting there as if he needed the contact.

Sounds of the steady downpour came in through the open window. She could smell the pungent scents of damp earth and wet greenery. Tomorrow everything would be revived and refreshed, the colours brilliant.

Tomorrow.

Sanity returned, blowing in on the rain-damp breeze that cooled her heated face. All the joy left her and anger and terror surfaced.

She'd been stupid, stupid, to let this happen. This was no way to get over an obsession. She slipped off the bed, grabbed her clothes and walked out of the room to her own. Was this the way it happened? Madness took hold of you and there was no defence? Like a demon taking over the controls of the brain? It was a terrifying thought indeed.

She took a cool shower, adjusting the nozzle to give a hard, stinging spray. Needles of water attacked her body, as if to exorcise the demon. Her skin began to tingle. 'Stupid, stupid, stupid,' she muttered to herself. 'Stupid, stupid, stupid.' Words dancing to an internal rhythm of fear and pain.

Somebody had put a curse on her, a malignant plot to keep her from finding happiness by having her fall in love with the wrong men forever and ever. Her entire life wasted with fruitless passions and desolate nights.

She dried herself with a big jade-coloured towel, wrapped it around herself and walked into her bedroom.

Max was standing by the window, dressed in white shorts and a blue shirt. 'We need to talk, Katrina,' he stated. So cool, so calm.

'It was a mistake,' she said huskily. Oh, God, she didn't feel up to this now.

He shoved his hands into his pockets, his face grim. 'No, it was not a mistake. We need each other, Katrina. You know that.'

She shook her head, her heart in her throat. 'No, no. We can't go on like this! It's all wrong! It was wrong from the beginning!'

His eyes held hers. 'What is wrong with me loving you, Katrina?'

He loved her. She felt her heart contract in anguish. He had never said that before, yet it didn't make things better—it made them worse.

'It won't work.' Her voice was squeaky. She took a deep breath, trying to calm herself, trying not to burst into tears. Standing there with nothing more than a towel wrapped around her didn't boost her self-confidence and dignity. She clenched her hands by her side. 'You're the wrong man for me, Max.'

His face went rigid. His mouth was a hard, angry line. He came towards her, stood still inches away from her, but didn't touch her. 'Then who is the right man? Tell me!'

She anchored her trembling legs to the floor. 'I don't know!'

Blue fire burned in his eyes. 'You know what your problem is, Katrina? You watch too many Doris Day movies!'

She glared at him. 'Are you telling me I'm out of touch with reality? If anybody knows about reality, it's me! I learned the hard way, so don't you dare analyse me!'

'Oh, but I will,' he said, his voice low. 'What you need to learn, Katrina, is to trust a little.'

'I did that once, and see what that got me!' She felt hysteria build up and it frightened her, yet she seemed unable to get herself under control. She was shaking all over. 'I told you, you are not the right man for me and I mean it! I don't want you!'

He towered over her, his piercing blue eyes boring into hers. 'The hell you don't,' he said.

The next day he was gone.

Her heart in her throat, she looked at the empty rooms. The computer gone, the photographs gone, all the books and papers gone. She could not believe it. According to

Mrs Blackett he had left that morning while Katrina was
at the orphanage reading to the children.

A note lay on the kitchen table.

Katrina, In the circumstances I think I'm doing us
both a favour by leaving. Thank you for the use of
your house, your delicious meals, and your help with
the creative process. Max.

She crumpled the note and threw it on top of the
mango peels in the waste basket. Good riddance, she
thought. She had the house to herself again. No more
blue eyes to make her heart go berserk. No more phone
calls from the Parasite Sisters. No more Cassandras. No
more Isabel.

No more arms to hold her and make her feel treasured
and loved.

She rushed up the stairs to her room, stripped off her
clothes, got into the shower and wept. The sooner she
got rid of all the tears, the sooner she could start over.

She worked like a maniac every day. With the meagre
remnants of her former fortune she bought a piece of
land, had it cleared and levelled, had materials brought
out from Barbados and Miami, hired workmen to build
the mesh and screen shade-houses. It was all going won-
derfully well.

So why did she feel so miserable?

It wasn't fair. She'd already had her share of misery
in her marriage with Bastian. She didn't deserve any
more. She deserved some friendly spirits to lighten her
heart and help her feel joy in her life. No friendly spirits
stood in line for the job.

She thought about Max every minute of the day.

'I am *not* Bastian,' he had said. The sentence came
back to her time and again. 'I am *not* Bastian.' Well,

that was true, wasn't it? He was handsome, famous, rich, and pursued by women, just like Bastian. But there the similarities stopped. Bastian had never worked a day in his life; Max earned his money the hard way. Bastian had happily accommodated his female fans; Max moved to an obscure island to get rid of them. Bastian had used people to serve his own selfish desires; Max loved and took care of the people in his life. When Bastian had made love to her, he'd left her empty and untouched; when Max made love to her he filled her up heart and soul.

'What you need to learn, Katrina, is to trust a little.'

So why was she here alone on the island? What evil spirit had taken possession of her now, scrambling her brain, her common sense, her emotions?

CHAPTER ELEVEN

THREE weeks and an eternity of misery later, a package was delivered to the villa. The sender was Max, the address his house in Vermont. Katrina stared at the address and her heart turned over in her chest. With trembling hands she ripped the paper off. It was a photocopy of Max's manuscript, a stack of loose sheets, heavy, intriguing. A note lay on top.

As promised, a copy of the manuscript for you to read. If you take offence at any of it, let me know before you sue me.

There was the title page, then another page with a dedication.

'For Katrina, my inspiration, my love.'

Tears welled up in her eyes and she wiped them away impatiently. Since when had she, Katrina MacKenzie, turned into a sentimental slob? It was degrading!

She took the box with her to the veranda and settled herself in a chair. She might as well get this over with. And if there was anything, *anything* at all that she didn't like, she would sue him. She had promised him.

She began to read.

Minutes later she was lost in another world, entranced and enthralled. It was a rough, tough story, full of danger and adventure and intrigue, full of rugged, ruthless men. It was a story stewed in humour and irony, written from an off-centre viewpoint, and she loved it. She cried and laughed while she read. She was there, seeing, feeling, tasting. She could see the craggy faces, hear the gritty voices. The men were hard and cynical. They'd lost money, loved ones and parts of their bodies. The women were bitter and disillusioned. They'd lost all their dreams, their hopes and their virtue.

Except Isabel.

It was Isabel who saved the hero, not to speak of the reader, from plunging into deep despair about the human condition. With her warmth, her love, her humour she was an example of all that was good. She imbued the story with a sense of hope for humanity and a joy of living. She was the lighted candle in a dark room, the smell of baking bread in a cosy cottage, the crackling fire on a snowy night.

Isabel was warm and generous and loving. She had short hair, ate Belgian chocolates, read romance novels and read stories to orphaned children. Isabel loved cooking and brewing up magic herbal potions and watching Doris Day movies and she loved the hero, who had lost an arm and had a terrible disposition.

Ah, Isabel! Survivor of her own tragedies. Strong, determined, with the indomitable will to live and be happy. Isabel, who found the last tiny spark of humanity in the deep, dark soul of the hero and fanned it into a roaring fire. And the hot flames destroyed the cynicism and bitterness and anger, magically transforming the hero into a warm, loving person, a passionate, generous lover—in short, a dream man.

It was not difficult to recognise bits of herself, bits of Max, bits of their relationship, all neatly camouflaged by the scenery of a different world. It was not difficult to understand what Max had tried to do.

It was three in the morning when she finally finished the book, having barely taken time to eat. She sat on top of her bed, hugging the manuscript to her breast and smiled to herself, seeing in her mind the words of his dedication: 'For Katrina, my inspiration, my love.' Oh, Max, she thought, I love you and there isn't a thing I can do about it. How can I fight magic? Why did I ever think I could?

The next morning she went into Port Royal and sent him a telegram: 'THE BOOK IS GREAT AND I'VE DECIDED NOT TO SUE YOU.'

A telegram was delivered the next day. 'THANK YOU,' was all it said.

She sighed and sent him another telegram: 'I'M HAVING A PARTY. YOU'RE INVITED.'

'I DON'T LIKE PARTIES,' he wrote back. 'TOO MANY FEMALES MAKING A NUISANCE OF THEMSELVES.'

'NO OTHER WOMEN INVITED,' she wrote back.

He stood in front of her two days later, tall and devastating, blue eyes blazing. Her heart lurched, then galloped for joy. It had only been a few weeks since she had seen him last, but he seemed more handsome now than she remembered, his face more square, his shoulders broader. He emanated power and virility.

She opened her mouth to say something, but the next moment she was crushed against him and he was kissing her like a man possessed.

'I can't live this way any more,' he groaned. The words seemed torn from his soul.

'What way?' she asked breathlessly. He was holding her so tight that she could barely breathe. If he didn't let up, she might just die in his arms.

'Without you. I want you with me. All the time.' He looked into her eyes, a look of desperation.

'All the time?' she said, swallowing hard.

'I can't seem to function without you,' he said. 'All I think of is you and how much I want you with me. I followed you to New York because the house here was so empty without you. I don't want any other woman, Katrina, only you, for the rest of my life. Please marry me.'

Her heart made a somersault in her breast. She'd not been prepared for this and she felt suddenly overwhelmed with both fear and joy. 'You said you had enough females in your life making you miserable.' Four half-sisters, a mother, and a grandmother.

'I'll marry them off, send them on a slow boat to China; I'll think of something.'

She swallowed hard. 'What about the Cassandras in your life?'

'I'll wave my ring at them and tell them I'm married and don't fool around. And if they dare come and disturb the peace here I'll throw them off the island.' Spoken like a real man.

'What you need to learn, Katrina, is to trust a little.' The remembered words rang in her head.

Her heart flowed over. 'I love you,' she said. The words came out, just like that. They bubbled up from her soul like a beautiful miracle, true and shining.

'I hoped you'd say that one day,' he said huskily.

'Well, it isn't easy,' she murmured. She simply couldn't help herself. 'You're a dream man only part of the time. The other part you're pretty unbearable.'

'Well, you know what my grandmother said: perfect is boring.' He kissed her again. 'I love you,' he said against her mouth. 'I love you more than I ever thought I'd be able to love any woman. All I want is to be with you and to have you around, to know you are there, somewhere near. I want to sleep with you and eat with you and spend the rest of my life with you.'

Magic words that brought tears to her eyes, balm for a soul that had been lonely and unloved for too long.

He gave a low moan. 'Please, don't cry,' he said, tightening his arms around her again. 'Am I being too possessive? Is marrying me such a distressing idea?'

'No, no!' She smiled through her tears. 'I think it's a perfect idea.'

'I know it's not going to be easy. I go through these periods of creative insanity that make people around me crazy. I'm a difficult person to live with.'

She had noticed.

She lifted her face to his and smiled bravely. 'Not for someone who loves you,' she said, which was a lie, but only a small one. Life wasn't going to be perfect. No one's life was. But perfect was boring and their love would last because it was real and full of magic.

And that was the truth.

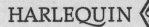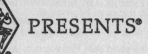

MILLION DOLLAR SWEEPSTAKES (III)

No purchase necessary. To enter, follow the directions published. Method of entry may vary. For eligibility, entries must be received no later than March 31, 1996. No liability is assumed for printing errors, lost, late or misdirected entries. Odds of winning are determined by the number of eligible entries distributed and received. Prizewinners will be determined no later than June 30, 1996.

Sweepstakes open to residents of the U.S. (except Puerto Rico), Canada, Europe and Taiwan who are 18 years of age or older. All applicable laws and regulations apply. Sweepstakes offer void wherever prohibited by law. Values of all prizes are in U.S. currency. This sweepstakes is presented by Torstar Corp., its subsidiaries and affiliates, in conjunction with book, merchandise and/or product offerings. For a copy of the Official Rules send a self-addressed, stamped envelope (WA residents need not affix return postage) to: MILLION DOLLAR SWEEPSTAKES (III) Rules, P.O. Box 4573, Blair, NE 68009, USA.

EXTRA BONUS PRIZE DRAWING

No purchase necessary. The Extra Bonus Prize will be awarded in a random drawing to be conducted no later than 5/30/96 from among all entries received. To qualify, entries must be received by 3/31/96 and comply with published directions. Drawing open to residents of the U.S. (except Puerto Rico), Canada, Europe and Taiwan who are 18 years of age or older. All applicable laws and regulations apply; offer void wherever prohibited by law. Odds of winning are dependent upon number of eligible entries received. Prize is valued in U.S. currency. The offer is presented by Torstar Corp., its subsidiaries and affiliates in conjunction with book, merchandise and/or product offering. For a copy of the Official Rules governing this sweepstakes, send a self-addressed, stamped envelope (WA residents need not affix return postage) to: Extra Bonus Prize Drawing Rules, P.O. Box 4590, Blair, NE 68009, USA.

SWP-H395

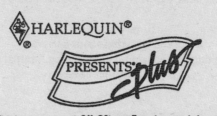

Harlequin invites you to the most
romantic wedding of the season.

Rope the cowboy of your dreams in
Marry Me, Cowboy!

A collection of 4 brand-new stories,
celebrating weddings, written by:

New York Times bestselling author

JANET DAILEY

and favorite authors

Margaret Way
Anne McAllister
Susan Fox

Be sure not to miss Marry Me, Cowboy!
coming this April

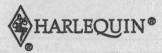

If you enjoyed this book by

CAROLE MORTIMER

Here's your chance to order more stories by one of
Harlequin's favorite authors:

Harlequin Presents®

#11468	ROMANCE OF A LIFETIME	$2.89	☐
#11543	SAVING GRACE	$2.89	☐
#11559	THE JILTED BRIDEGROOM	$2.99	☐
#11583	PRIVATE LIVES	$2.99	☐
#11607	MOTHER OF THE BRIDE	$2.99	☐
#11631	ELUSIVE OBSESSION	$2.99	☐
#11689	FATED ATTRACTION	$2.99 U.S.	☐
		$3.50 CAN.	☐
#11703	HUNTER'S MOON	$2.99 U.S.	☐
		$3.50 CAN.	☐

(limited quantities available on certain titles)

TOTAL AMOUNT	$
POSTAGE & HANDLING	$
($1.00 for one book, 50¢ for each additional)	
APPLICABLE TAXES*	$_____
TOTAL PAYABLE	$_____

(check or money order—please do not send cash)

To order, complete this form and send it, along with a check or money order
for the total above, payable to Harlequin Books, to: **In the U.S.:** 3010 Walden
Avenue, P.O. Box 9047, Buffalo, NY 14269-9047; **In Canada:** P.O. Box 613,
Fort Erie, Ontario, L2A 5X3.

Name: _____

Address: _____ City: _____

State/Prov.: _____ Zip/Postal Code: _____

*New York residents remit applicable sales taxes.
Canadian residents remit applicable GST and provincial taxes.   HCMBACK3

◆ HARLEQUIN®